PR

THE SECRETS WE CONCEAL

"The Secrets We Conceal is an incredible story of grit, perseverance, and bravery. This story is devastating, raw, and romantic in one. The Secrets We Conceal is a must-read that you can't put down."
Dana Derricks, 12 – Time Award-Winning Author

In her debut novel, The Secrets We Conceal, S. R. Fabrico writes openly, honestly, and delicately about the difficult subject of child sexual abuse. By showing, not telling, this story reminds readers that childhood trauma does not simply go away in adulthood—rather, it has long-lasting effects on the developing brain and body. The power and pain of Laura's story will stay with me for a long time. I'm still cheering for Laura and all of the survivors she represents. I give the book five stars.
Tracy Stopler MS, RD Award-winning author, The Ropes That Bind

"As a therapist in practice for over 20 years, treating female abuse and trauma, The Secrets We Conceal is a story that countless numbers of young girls can relate to. The trauma narrative, in the beginning, is hard to get through, even as a trained EMDR trauma therapist. However, this story of how the universe sends love to conquer evil is a redemptive message of hope and speaks to human resilience. It is my hope that this book will land in the hands of other women who might have suffered like the main character and that they will be empowered to speak out and find their own healing. A must-read for anyone that feels they are at the end of their rope. The reader will cry tears of sadness, joy and laughter at this tragically witty story where in the end love really does conquer all evil. "

Sarah R. Coates, M.Ed, LCMHC, NCC

"A haunting tale of innocence being stripped from a young girl, but with the power of finding confidence and self-worth. Profoundly moving while shedding light on an important social issue that every parent needs to pay attention to. A must-read for any parent/caregiver who wants to feel empowered to have an open conversation with their child to keep them protected or allowing them to have a voice."

SDC, Mother of a young pre-teen daughter

"S.R. Fabrico has created a book where we can find unexpected messages about ourselves and the world around us. I resonated with the main character, Laura, and the journey that she overcame. Her story is full of moments that change lives and while my story is different from hers, some commonalities brought pain yet also brought the feeling that I could share my journey and struggles. I cried, laughed, and loved this book, it is a must-read!"

M.W., Survivor

"I must say, the pages were both tearful and inspiring. This is quite a story. It is raw, romantic, and terrifying all in one. It meant the world to me to be part of bringing this book to life."

James Austin, Author

"I think The Secrets We Conceal is really well written and I love the story. To be honest, I couldn't put it down and trust me, this doesn't happen often for me."

Amy Bennett, Editor and Proofreader

"I absolutely loved this book! It's so raw, sad, and real. My heart was pounding and breaking in so many places. The writing style really connects you with the characters, making the emotions so real."

S. Graham, Author of Vacant

THE SECRETS
WE CONCEAL

S. R. Fabrico

S.R. FABRICO

For my incredible husband, my soulmate, Chris.
I am forever grateful to have you by my side.

I love you!

PROLOGUE

Her joints refused to move even while she commanded them to and her heartbeat pounded hard and wild against her ribcage. With her back against the bed and her eyes fixated on the ceiling, Laura tried to catch her breath. Sweat flowed down her face, oozed out from every pore of her body, and soaked her bed.

"It's just a dream," she thought she heard herself say. "It was just a bad dream."

Realizing the strong and supportive tone was not her voice, Laura finally turned her head toward the left. "He" smiled and reached for her with his warm hands and firm, calming grip.

"I'm here, babe," he said. "Nothing is going to harm you. I'm right here, and I'll always be here."

His words were believable, and his eyes shone not of the demons she had seen in her dream but of kindness, love, and purity. His touch seemed to cast every fright consuming her body into nonexistence. He wrapped himself slowly around her and gently moved her head to rest on his chest. Right until that moment, she had no idea just how scared he had been for her. His raging heartbeats gave his fear away, yet the man heroically gathered enough strength for her and continued to whisper assuring words.

"He'll never lay a finger on you again," he promised.

She believed every word he had said. The tone and manner he had spoken the words were genuine, as they had been for the twenty-four years they had been together.

Laura sighed and wiped off the tears from her eyes and the sweat that still drenched her face before whispering, "I love you, Tom."

Tom nodded with a smile, leaned closer, and planted a kiss on her forehead before holding her tightly in his arms. For Laura, she had felt the demons from her childhood sneak back into her subconscious through the night. Laura remembered the devil in human flesh and the evil deeds he committed against her when she was a child. She could never rid herself of those past experiences and betrayal. No matter how hard she tried, it seemed a small piece of shame and darkness still lingered and ate away at her soul.

She was glad it was nothing but a terrible dream. There was no way he would be able to get her now. She wasn't that vulnerable little girl anymore, and more importantly, she had Tom now.

ONE

Fall 1985

L aura, excited about her visit that day with her cousin Susie, danced and jumped around the living room that morning. Laura's house had a lot of rules and expectations. There was always cleaning to do, leaves to rake, or vegetables to pick. At Susie's house, they sat around and watched TV and could run and play all they wanted. Susie's parents would get them fast food biscuits and hash browns in the morning. Laura never liked the pulpy orange juice, but they would buy some of that too. The only time she ever ate fast food or drank soda was at Susie's.

Laura's mother, Samantha, hurried into the living room excitedly and said, "I just called your Aunt Penny, kiddo, and you're all set to stay with her and Susie." They had not informed Laura, but there was a possibility that they wouldn't return home for the night. "Just in case we don't make it home early enough, we'll plan to pick you up tomorrow morning," her mother explained with a promise.

"It will be fun for you girls." Laura hurried to her room to pack an overnight bag.

She rummaged through her messy closet floor and looked for her shiny bright pink bag with the ballerina slippers appliqué stitched onto the front. Laura loved that bag. She remembered wanting that bag so much; it was the proper bag for a budding ballerina. She squealed with glee when she found the bag. She pulled back the zipper and dumped out her dance shoes so she could pack a few things for her overnight stay.

Laura understood little about her parents' trip, but she had heard her father mention something about visiting some friends near the shore. Her parents loved to travel. Since Laura's siblings were 13 and 14 years older than her, they had moved out of the house years ago, so it was just Laura at home. An only child of sorts, but not.

She gave some more thought to the fun things she would love to do once she got to her cousin's house. She brought her packed bag out to the kitchen, where Samantha was cleaning up.

Pushing her luck, Laura asked, "Can I stay up and watch TV tonight?"

Samantha looked at her, shook her head, and said, "I expect you to be on your best behavior when you get to their house, and you can only watch what your Aunt Penny and Uncle Max let you girls watch, okay?"

Her mom's reply was a letdown of sorts, but it was no bother for Laura, and she hurried out the door. She knew her Aunt Penny and Uncle Max were far laxer in their judgments and actions than her parents were. She helped herself into the back seat of their powder blue Mercedes and fastened her seatbelt while she waited for her parents. They needed a few more minutes to get ready, but Laura didn't mind the wait because her time at Susie's would be perfect. The day seemed ideal, and the prospect of spending time with her cousin Susie was exciting.

A bit impatient, Laura counted the minutes as they rolled by until her father, Paul, finally slipped into the driver's seat and started the engine. The radio blared to the tune of Elvis Presley. Laura's feet started tapping, and her dad's head began bobbing. *Blue Suede Shoes* blared from the speakers as he pulled out of the driveway. Laura barely looked back at the house. She couldn't wait to go to her cousin's house that day.

***

Samantha got out of the car and helped Laura out from the backseat. They both watched as Paul tried to park the car perfectly beside the tan and brown station wagon and the navy-blue Trans Am. The Trans Am was Uncle Max's prized possession. He adored that car; it was a kind of status symbol. In his mind, he was a big shot when he drove it. Laura stared at the three-bedroom yellow rancher that belonged to her Aunt Penny's mom. Uncle Max had just returned from active-duty training at Fort Dix. He needed some time to get back on his feet, so they were living there temporarily. The house had an odd front porch and no fence surrounding the yard.

Aunt Penny had a tri-colored beagle who huffed and puffed while yanking at its chain as it tried to pull itself free. Uncle Max and Aunt Penny didn't like to walk the dog, so he remained tied up to a stake in the yard most of the day. The poor boy barked loudly and made a nuisance of himself to the neighbors, obviously in displeasure at not being allowed to roam free. Laura approached the house slowly, hearing the dog growl, but she was used to it. She felt sorry for the dog. He was either in the small house or tied to the chain with no place to run free.

Laura skipped up the steps leading to the porch and opened the door without realizing how fast the storm door swung back in place. It clipped her right ankle bringing her great stinging pain.

"Be careful, girlie!" Aunt Penny rushed over with her sweet and caring voice before looking at the sore spot on Laura's ankle.

Laura squirmed in pain as Aunt Penny used her hand to rub some relief into her ankle.

"Where's Susie?" Laura asked.

Susie smiled and came running over to Laura with her arms open wide. They had not seen each other in what felt like years, but only a few months had passed since Susie last visited Laura's house for a weekend. Aunt Penny let go of Laura's foot, and the pain radiating from her sore ankle started to fade.

"Hey girls," Aunt Penny mumbled with a thin smile as she turned to Laura's parents standing on the front porch. "Samantha!" Aunt Penny wrapped her arms around her sister-in-law before pulling away and sharing a second hug with Paul. The family relationship was always confusing to Laura. Aunt Penny was actually her dad's niece. She couldn't understand how that was possible; her dad and Aunt Penny were practically the same age. Paul said that Penny and Max were Laura's elders, and she should call them Aunt Penny and Uncle Max, but she supposed they were really her cousins.

"I wasn't expecting you two this early."

"Thank you for keeping our girl for the night," Samantha said to Aunt Penny as they walked inside the house and Susie and Laura raced towards the living room. The air inside smelled stale, mixed with the dog's awful stench. The dog needed a bath. Susie looked around for a comfortable spot to sit amidst the TV trays scattered around the living room. The foul-smelling carpet made Laura's stomach sink every time; indeed, the entire house always seemed dirty, which made her uncomfortable sitting just about anywhere.

Samantha insisted their house be immaculate. "Everything has its place," she would say, so Laura wasn't used to a cluttered home.

Regardless of the condition of the house, she was happy to spend time with her cousin. Aunt Penny went into the kitchen to get the girls a plate of chocolate chip cookies while she spoke to Laura's parents. The kitchen sink was full of last night's dinner dishes, and take-out breakfast trash littered the counter.

Penny turned to Samantha and said, "Of course, Samantha, we're happy to have her."

"Look at who we've got here!" the coarse, spine-tingling voice echoed as the front door opened and a tall, burly fellow with receding grey hair came in smiling at the girls.

Jumping to her feet, Susie cried aloud, "Daddy!"

Laura followed with a warm hug as she wrapped her arms around her Uncle Max. The girls walked with him while he ran his fingers through their hair. Donning his usual white undershirt and military-style shorts bearing old stains and a dour look as though it craved to get washed, he pulled them close to his body, each of them on either side of him.

Laura looked up into his face, and he stared back at her with an odd smile she had never seen on him before. He rarely smiled and wore a plain expression most of the time.

"Look who showed up earlier than we expected," Aunt Penny said to Uncle Max.

"Hey Max, it's good to see you," Paul said as he shook the man's hand firmly before sharing a brief bro-hug with him. "How's Joey doing?" Joey was Uncle Max's son from a previous marriage.

"He's doing well, we don't see him much since he moved to California," Uncle Max said proudly. "Your daughter has quickly grown into a fine young lady. It almost feels like yesterday when she used to crawl around the house making a mess of my things."

Samantha laughed and said, "Well, they grow pretty fast, don't they?"

Aunt Penny looked at Uncle Max and said, "Laura's staying with us for the night. Samantha and Paul will pick her up in the morning."

Uncle Max looked at Laura and then looked back at his wife. "No problem at all. She can stay here for as long as she wants."

The adults caught up on old times and sealed the deal with a beer.

***

Susie and Laura sat glued to the TV with Uncle Max, although Laura couldn't have cared less about the show. She couldn't quite wrap her young mind around what the Chuck Norris movie was all about. There were ramblings and endless use of swear words that her parents would never approve of. Although Susie didn't appear to enjoy the movie either, she barely flinched; the language seemed common to her.

Laura looked up at her Uncle Max, whose eyes darted intermittently from the TV to Laura, and he caught sight of her every time she looked his way. He seemed unable to help himself. His gleaming eyes sent chills down her young spine. She was old enough to know his stares felt odd but not old enough to understand beyond those uncomfortable feelings.

"You girls should come sit with me," Uncle Max said soon after they had found a comfortable spot on a scarce but neat place on the carpet.

Susie leaped from her spot first, while Laura wasn't entirely jubilant about sitting with Uncle Max. Flanking the man on either side, Laura to his left and Susie to his right, something about the way he adjusted and pulled them closer gave her that odd feeling again. Even with her innocent little brain, she knew that something didn't feel right.

"How old are you now, Laura?" Uncle Max asked.

Laura looked up at him with her childish grin and replied, "Nine."

He let out a fake gasp and widened his eyes and said, "Nine? You and Susie are such big girls already."

He reached his arm around Laura, aiming for her ribs, and tickled her, which caused her to squirm and loosen up a bit. She relaxed at that moment and thought, *you are just a little girl, what do you know? He is your uncle, someone to be trusted*, and brushed aside her previous feelings.

Laura giggled through his tickles, and said, "Mom calls me her baby."

Susie looked up at her father and then looked away. She turned her gaze back to the TV as time ticked by slowly around them. Uncle Max sat calmly as he moved his eyes from the TV to the girls and back to the TV. As they sat in silence on either side, the uneasy feeling crept back into Laura's belly.

Susie had gotten up and raced to the kitchen to get herself something to drink when Uncle Max put his hand on Laura's back.

"Let's play a game," he said. "I'll draw a word on your back, and you try to guess what it is."

That seems fun, Laura thought.

"T-O-Y-S. Toys." Laura said with confidence.

"Good job, let's do another."

Uncle Max spelled a few more words, but eventually, his hand moved in an oscillatory motion that led from the upper part towards the lower end of her spine. Laura simply adjusted, squirming like she had an itch on her back as she tried not to acknowledge his hand. The creepy feeling in her gut had escalated and throbbed rhythmically. With her hair standing up on edge, Laura had retreated to a conversation in her head, one voice screamed alarm and the other voice told her to calm down. *He's your uncle, a man you can trust, a man you're supposed to respect. Be on your best behavior. It's just a game, Laura.* Grappling with so many thoughts swirling in her head, she was startled back to earth in the tiny living room from a voice in the kitchen.

"Do you want some chocolate ice cream?" Susie called aloud.

Looking for any excuse to get up, Laura jumped out of Max's arms and ran toward the kitchen. She could hear Uncle Max grumble underneath his breath as she escaped from his grasp. Susie could have offered her a dog turd, and she would have gone running like it was the most delicious food on the planet.

"Where'd your mom go?" Laura asked Susie.

"She went to the grocery store to buy some things we need for dinner, but she'll be back soon."

Laura thought if she could just stay with Aunt Penny or Susie the rest of the day, she would be okay. She could breathe and sort this out in her head. Was she overreacting? *Be a good girl, it was just a game* she thought.

The girls helped themselves to a bowl of chocolate ice cream Aunt Penny left for them in case they were hungry. Within a minute of digging out the last scoop, Uncle Max yelled out, "You girls get back here. You don't need to eat more junk!"

Surprised and frightened by his tone, Laura motioned for them to head back. Uncle Max had straightened up in his seat and, with angry-looking eyes, stared uncomfortably at them.

"We're supposed to hang out and have fun together," he said. "Don't worry, Aunt Penny will be back soon, and we'll eat some dinner."

"Susie," Uncle Max called out again to his daughter, "get me a beer from the fridge, will you?"

Susie grabbed the Coors from the refrigerator, and the girls walked back to sit into the living room. This time, Laura sat on the floor; she thought the nasty carpet would be safer than the couch. Susie handed the beer to her dad and announced she'd be right back, "Gotta go to the bathroom," she said as she walked out of the room. Alone with Uncle Max in the living room, Laura sensed the uncomfortable feeling shoot through her stomach once again. The uneasy feeling escalated through most of her body as Uncle Max came to sit on the floor next to her. His hand reached for her back again. He slowly raised her shirt this time and ran his rough and hardened palm along her spine. Laura moved and squirmed, but he wouldn't stop.

She never had such a feeling when her father rubbed her back or ran his hand through her hair when they watched TV, but Uncle Max's touch felt different. His slow caresses made Laura feel queasy. His hand was cold and scratchy, her body was tense, and screamed inside that his hand should not be there. She was like an animal cornered with nowhere to go. What was she supposed to do? Call out? To whom?

Laura froze in a mixture of emotions, mostly fear, as she endured his hand reaching farther down her back. She tried to fixate her thoughts towards the TV in hopes he might stop soon. He didn't. She looked around the room and hoped to find something to distract herself. Laura noticed the family picture that hung on the wall wrapped in a shiny gold frame. She noticed the Avon catalog on the end table. She loved to look through the book with her cousin. They would always choose several items they would never actually buy, but they had a great time pretending. Her eyes then drifted down to the brown shag carpet that never seemed vacuumed; she could almost see the fleas jumping through the air. The minutes felt like forever, but finally, she could hear Susie coming back down the hallway. *Relief*, Laura thought.

Uncle Max mumbled something about his military training, but she had no interest in his tale. Instead, she wanted his hand to stop moving along her bare skin and underneath her shirt. Laura moved her body in a different direction to have him ease off, but he wouldn't, and every attempt only made him intensify his effort. Surely, he would stop as Susie entered the living room. But she kept waiting and wondering, *where did she go?*

She sighed intermittently, he reeked of beer, which threatened to suffocate her little lungs the longer she stayed in his reach.

He reached for his half-drunk can sitting on top of the TV tray, downed it, and wiped the drops of beer on his chin with his shirt. Laura prayed. She hoped he would get up and go for another beer or perhaps go to the bathroom to relieve his bladder.

Her prayers went unanswered.

His hands felt like wood brushing against her skin. Slowly and relentlessly, he progressed from simply running his hand along her back to circling her waistline. She struggled to move his hand off, while he rubbed her belly button for a few seconds before he reached towards her yet-to-be-developed breasts to toy with her nipple gently. She hoped she was confused, that perhaps her Uncle Max's hand landed there by accident. It was Laura's nine-year-old way of trying to rationalize what has just happened to her.

She could hear him moan softly but she didn't understand what the sounds meant and why his hands just wouldn't leave her body. The thought to scream out to Susie crossed her mind, but she felt too scared to do so. The ongoing Chuck Norris movie only seemed to echo her fears, trying to figure out what exactly her Uncle Max was doing to her. Laura was a child, powerless and afraid. She felt enraged, sad, and confused all at the same time. She knew she couldn't sit there anymore.

Coaxing herself from the inside out, Laura mustered up the courage to be brave, to stand tall, to do something, anything.

"I need to go," she mumbled finally.

He refused and pulled her closer as though he wouldn't allow her to break free. He continued and rubbed her chest mildly as he lingered his fingers atop her nipples. Her body squirmed to get free now, but Laura was no match for him, and he made sure to position her body well enough to prevent her from escaping.

Then, like a miracle, came the sound of a car parking just outside the house, and Uncle Max quickly pulled his hand from underneath Laura's shirt. She sighed in relief and tried to forget her Uncle Max's sickening behavior before she raced to the window to see if Aunt Penny had returned.

"Susie, Susie, your mom's back!" Laura turned around excitedly and cried aloud. Susie suddenly appeared from nowhere. Laura drew closer to her cousin, "Where were you?" Susie stared back at her with a frown and didn't reply.

Aunt Penny's face pleaded for assistance as she struggled to open the storm door. Breathing hard and sweating profusely, she finally made her entrance with her arms full of grocery bags. Max simply tuned to another channel, crossed his legs, and laughed out loud while he entertained himself by watching Sam Malone and Norm banter back and forth on *Cheers*.

Aunt Penny slowly made her way into the kitchen. She looked like she had fought through hell to get the groceries. She looked worn out. Her spiky-dyed dark black hair erupted from her head, and her shirt had become half untucked from her sizable waistband.

"I'm hungry," Uncle Max said from where he sat, taking a sip from a newly opened beer.

Laura rolled her eyes at his words while Susie hurried to help her mother. As the duo struggled to get the bags unpacked, Laura ran over to help them. They worked together to put away the groceries, stacking the cold items on the counter and the dry goods on the table for Aunt Penny to put away. Susie gathered all the grocery bags to place them under the sink for future use.

Aunt Penny slowly walked to the rocking chair in the living room and planted herself in it, while Susie and Laura followed, finding a seat on the floor. Aunt Penny looked drained, sweaty, and barely able to catch her breath. Uncle Max guzzled the new beer bottle and rolled it underneath the couch. The clanking sound indicated the bottle had struck another, prompting the question of just how many bottles might be underneath the old couch. The four of them sat for at least an hour quietly watching TV.

"Dinner will be ready soon," Aunt Penny sighed, getting to her feet, and dragging them as she headed to the kitchen.

Uncle Max stretched and yawned before putting his feet on the couch as he continued with his movie. Susie and Laura went to help Aunt Penny in the kitchen, Laura was content to stay in there for the rest of the evening until dinner was ready.

Two

D inner was good, but not as perfect as having it with her parents. Although Laura couldn't wait to spend time with her cousin, all she could think about now was being home. She did enjoy her meal though and the chocolate cheesecake her Aunt Penny had purchased from the store. Uncle Max started his meal in silence away from the dinner table, which was the norm at their house.

Their family's norm was apparent when Susie came to Laura's home. She wanted to eat in the living room in front of the TV, but she joined the family at the kitchen table, which was the rule at Laura's house. Laura didn't care for her parents' rules, but now, she appreciated those expectations and longed to be with her parents in the safety and comfort of her home.

Uncle Max asked Laura to sit next to him on the couch and eat on the TV tray. She ignored him. He eventually moved to the dining table and sat next to Laura.

"This is odd," Aunt Penny joked, "Max, you hardly ever sit at the table." Laughing and joking, they continued to eat while Susie made fart noises with her armpits. Laura's mom would have slapped her out of her chair if she had done that. However, she welcomed the distraction. Her Aunt Penny, Uncle Max, and cousin Susie were all sitting together, for a moment, there was a brief glimmer of a happy family.

Laura watched her Aunt Penny clear the table while Susie helped her. She excused herself and headed for the bedroom. It didn't bother Laura that the chaos inside the room was in stark contrast to what she was used to. Instead, she wondered how great it must be to leave the room a mess. Susie's toys ranged from her wrestling collections to the Barbie dolls that had either been decapitated or left hanging absurdly from the bed.

Laura felt calmer than she had earlier. Uncle Max wasn't anywhere near her, so she could retreat to safety and solidarity in her cousin's room. She walked halfway down the hallway and shouted to her Aunt Penny and Susie that her stomach didn't feel so great, and she was going to shower and get ready for bed. She planned to sleep against the wall, tucked safely away in the corner of the room. She allowed her mind to wander to the events earlier in the day, but she didn't quite understand how to process what had happened. Laura also wasn't sure what to do. Who could she tell? *Susie*, she thought, or *maybe her Aunt Penny.* No, she'd wait and tell her mom tomorrow. The uneasy feeling rested in her gut; she was alone, confused, and hurting. Laura couldn't tell a soul. How could she? He was the adult, her Uncle Max, a military man, a man to be trusted. Who would believe her? They would be angry, so angry. How could she hurt Susie and Aunt Penny like that? After all, they were just playing a game, right? Maybe it was an innocent mistake.

Taking a moment to draw a breath while these thoughts swirled through her mind, she stared at the bathroom in fear. Laura closed her eyes and took a slow breath and tried to convince herself she had overreacted. Suddenly, the idea of being naked for even a fraction of time in this house terrified her. She preferred to wait until she got home to shower, however, Samantha would expect her to follow her normal routine. Her mother would expect her to wash and brush her teeth before they came to get her the next day. *I'll do it in the morning,* Laura thought.

Laura slipped out of her shirt and quickly took off her jeans before neatly folding them and laying them next to the bathroom sink. With a grimace sprawled across her face, she dug her pajamas out of the pink ballet bag and began to dress as quickly as possible. Scared stiff and terrified, she dressed so fast that she had put her pajama pants on backward.

She heard a noise, or she thought something moved, and her ears caught the sound. But she heard nothing else. Choosing to believe the noise was in her head, she flipped her pants around the correct way. She was glad to change her clothes. Fresh clean jammies were exactly what she needed to rid herself of the stench and dirt that must have clung to her clothes from sitting on the floor.

Laura had just turned around and looked at the door when a shadowy figure breezed past. Her heart threatened to leap into her throat, and her breath quickened as her pulse raced. She peeked through the crack in the door but saw nothing. She let out a sigh of relief. Certain she let her mind play tricks on her, she opened the door to an almost nerve-wracking discovery of Susie standing a few feet away.

"Oh my God!" Laura jumped.

Susie seemed perplexed by Laura's frightful look. "Are you okay?"

Unsure of how to respond, Laura simply nodded.

"I thought I saw someone standing and peeping through the door," Laura explained.

Susie shrugged and replied, "I just walked up after helping mom clean up in the kitchen."

Laura had no reason to doubt her cousin, she hurried to sit on the bed while Susie took her shower. She could not wait to have some playtime before Aunt Penny would order them both to bed. When Laura saw a box of toys lying at the foot of the closet, she hurried over and began unloading. She set aside the Lincoln Logs and Barbies and settled on a Cornsilk Cabbage Patch doll named Astra. She was brushing Astra's hair neatly with the pink plastic brush she also found in the box when suddenly she could feel her hair standing on the back of her neck. Laura sensed something had leaned close to the window, and she saw what looked like a face, but there was nothing, only the darkness that surrounded the moon as it burned brightly outside. She cast her gaze back to the doll, and her heart remained unsettled as it continued to beat hard against her ribcage. She resumed brushing Astra's hair just as Susie made her way out of the bathroom.

Re-entering the bedroom with a towel wrapped around her body, Laura asked her cousin, "What game do you want to play tonight?"

Susie turned around to the door, slammed it shut, locked it, then double-checked to make sure it was indeed locked. She walked over to the window and rolled down the blinds before turning to Laura and giggling without explaining her actions.

"We could play Uno," Susie finally answered while she picked out her nightgown and began dressing. Laura nodded and smiled. She attempted to get back to her feet and head towards the bed when a loud racket coming from the door caused her to trip and almost fall flat on her face. Someone was trying to force the door open by pulling hard on the knob.

"Susie! Susie!" They could hear Uncle Max's voice call from the other side of the door.

Susie looked frightened but did not attempt to respond.

"How many times have I warned you about having this door locked?" he shouted angrily.

Susie rushed to the door, unlocked it, and slowly retreated while her red-faced father stormed into the room and headed straight for the window to crack the blinds. He paused momentarily and glared at Susie before storming back out of the room, leaving the door open and a somewhat confused-looking Laura wondering what was going on.

Choosing to say nothing about the bizarre incident, she turned to Susie shuffling the cards, and said, "Let's play."

***

Laura opened her eyes to the startling sight of green khaki shorts and a brownish-looking white shirt. There was no guessing who they belonged to. Uncle Max's weird smirk greeted her warmly with his hand reaching for her face. The act brought back the feeling from the actions of the previous day.

Slowly, Laura sat up and rubbed her eyes. Clearing her throat, she motioned to greet Uncle Max. Her throat felt glued, and her words were somewhat shy to come out. His presence didn't feel right.

"You look so beautiful while you sleep," he whispered.

Nodding her head and staring blankly at her uncle, Laura replied, "Good morning, Uncle Max."

With his eyes glaring down at her, he barely blinked while his hand massaged the comforter gently. Drawing away from him slowly, Laura pulled the comforter closer to her body. She looked around the room and noticed an open drawer with clothes spilling out from it onto the floor. Susie was nowhere to be found.

"Where's Susie?" she asked, sounding nervous.

Uncle Max shrugged, reached for the comforter, and pulled it slowly off her body, revealing her bare neck. Hearing someone's footsteps approaching the room, he stopped suddenly.

Laura felt thankful but still wasn't entirely sure what was going on. She leaned, bearing her weight on her left shoulder, and caught a glimpse of Susie standing by the door with an uncomfortable expression all over her face.

Her fists clenched, and her eyes stared solely on the back of her father's head.

Innocently, Laura cried out for her cousin in excitement, "Susie, where were you?"

Susie cleared her throat and answered, "I felt a tickle in my throat and went to get some water."

Uncle Max still had not looked at his daughter, but suddenly a look of frustration covered his face. Sighing, he lowered his head carefully and let go of the comforter without his daughter noticing. He turned around and barely said a word to her as he exited the room.

"Are you okay?" Susie said in a worrisome tone.

Laura nodded and said, "Yes… I'm just hungry".

Tussling with each other playfully, the girls burst into laughter. Gasping and panting for air, Susie flopped into bed and remained silent before turning to look at Laura. Susie seemed lost in thought. Her usually vibrant persona seemed absent.

Susie said, "My mom is making breakfast. You need to clean up, pack your things, and come eat." Susie headed towards the dresser to begin shoving down some more clothes.

Laura slid out from underneath the comforter and stepped into her slippers. She felt her spine stiffen with a disturbing sense of anxiety, prompting her to retract cautiously. Her face was slowly oozing with sweat, and her mouth felt dry with worry as she looked at her cousin, who remained distracted by whatever she hoped to find in the dresser.

Marching through the mess of clothes littered around the floor, Laura headed out of the bedroom and down the short narrow hall to the bathroom and slammed the door shut. Stepping backward slowly she rammed the lock into place and felt herself heave out a loud sigh.

Her heart raced the moment she took her first step inside. The bathroom suddenly felt smaller and less private, even with the door closed behind her. She planned to brush her teeth first because she didn't need to pull off her clothes to do that.

Trapped between brushing, and casting her attention towards the locked door, her senses heightened and remained tuned towards hearing any strange sounds. She could hear Susie still straightening her mess a short distance down the hall.

"Laura!" Susie called out. "You sure are spending a lot of time in there!"

"I'll be out in a minute!" Laura was so lost in thought; she had not realized that she had spent almost 15-minutes brushing her teeth by the time she glanced at the watch strapped on her wrist.

She finally began to undress. An effortless task on a normal day suddenly became difficult to get done. Her breath became erratic as she stared at the door. She took off her pajamas and folded them neatly before tucking them in her bag. Finally, she stepped into the tub, turned the shower knob, and began to wash.

Take your shower and head to the living room for breakfast she practically sang to herself while she rubbed on some soap and set about her business.

Laura heard a click and then the bathroom door slowly opened with a creaking sound. Laura could feel herself almost jump out of her skin as she hurriedly washed the soap from her face.

Susie's head poked in, causing Laura to lose her grip on the soap and eventually drop it as her cousin spoke, "Breakfast is ready, and your food is going to get cold."

"You scared me!" Laura raged. "I'm almost done. I'll be right there!"

Susie slammed the door shut and left the room in a huff. Laura washed off quickly choosing not to wash her hair. She hopped out of the shower and hurried to dry off and get dressed. She couldn't shake the uneasy feeling she had in the house.

Laura wanted to eat breakfast, and she hoped her rush of anxiety would simmer away.

***

Breakfast was over, but Laura still felt anxious and uncomfortable. It had been two hours since her bathroom retreat, and even while she and Susie played with some of her remote-control cars, she couldn't help but tense when she heard a door open. She used to have a lot of fun at Susie's house. But since Uncle Max came back, and they moved into this house, things were different. Uncle Max's stories about "Nam," whatever that was, seemed to change him. He spent most of his time sitting in the living room and drinking.

Uncle Max walked over to where the girls were, kicked their toys, and looked at them with a frown. "Get those things out of here!"

Susie packed them up quickly and raced to her room to dump them onto the floor. Before Susie returned, Uncle Max walked past Laura and smiled at her, he reached for her cheeks and tugged at them gently. Laura took a sudden breath, only to smell the familiar stench of dog and beer. He had been drinking already, so early in the morning.

"You are really beautiful," he whispered.

Laura shyly retreated thinking, *he is always telling me how beautiful I am*. Normally a compliment would feel good, but from Uncle Max, the words brought a queasiness in her belly.

Susie appeared and looked at her father before asking, "Can we play outside? We promise not to go far."

"Okay, but you girls had better not mess with my car," he warned.

The words brought absolute joy to Susie, who immediately raced to the door and out of the house. Laura followed her cousin but winced as the storm door did what it did best, rammed into her foot and brought her pain. Regardless, she felt happy about leaving the confines of the house. The first breath of fresh air outside brought her insides some relief, and she smiled wildly.

Susie grabbed her purple kickball for the girls to play. They were never caged, but being outside felt good. The skies looked more beautiful, and the earth underneath her feet felt warm.

They ran around kicking and throwing the ball at each other. It was nice to be outside for a change, just the two of them. Getting a little short of breath, Susie paused for a moment and then headed to get the garden hose. Susie didn't exercise much, so it didn't take long for her to get winded. Laura looked through the weeds in the grass to find a four-leaf clover. Her grass at home didn't have anything resembling a four-leaf clover. She thought maybe if she could find one here, it would bring her some luck. She would gratefully take any kind of luck today.

Suddenly, cold splashing water jolted her out of her daze as Susie, wielding a hose in hand, sprayed her right in the face and down her shirt. Susie was drenched and intended to do the same to Laura. No sooner had Laura stood up to run away than a honking sound from an approaching car alerted Laura of her parents' arrival.

"Yippee!" she cried in excitement while Susie looked sad.

"I guess it is time for you to leave," Susie mumbled.

Laura turned to her before placing her hands on the girl's shoulders while their eyes connected and said, "I will be back soon to spend more time with you."

Susie believed her. If there was one thing about Laura that was always true, it was her sincerity and desire to spend time with her cousin as often as she could. Laura felt relieved about leaving the house, and while she promised to come back, it was something she would come to wish she had never done.

Standing by the window was Uncle Max, smiling and waving at her. He had been watching Susie and Laura drench themselves with the hose.

THREE

Summer – 1986

Laura woke up early because Wednesdays were for the seashore. Samantha, Aunt Penny, Susie, and Laura were going to drive to Brigantine Beach and spend the day. Laura was so excited. She loved the seashore and couldn't wait to get there. Crossing the room to her long white dresser, she practically sprang out of bed. Flinging open the bottom drawer, she shuffled through her bathing suits as she decided which one to wear. At first, she tried on her favorite pink and white bikini with bright pink bottoms and a pink and white gingham halter top. She checked herself in the mirror and decided she wasn't tan enough to wear the bikini. Her olive skin didn't burn too easily, but this would be her first day in the sun all summer. She had weeks of beach days to go and thought it might be best to wear something else. Laura continued digging through her drawers and came across a black swim top her mom gave her last summer. *Yes, perfect*, she thought to herself, *I will wear my bikini, and I will bring my swim top too.* She reached in her closet and grabbed her terrycloth coverup to throw over her suit, slipped her feet in her brand-new flip flops, and sat at her vanity to fix her hair.

She could practically smell the salt air as she brushed her long brown locks. The sound of the waves, the sun on her skin, and the sand in her toes filled her with excitement and anticipation. Laura fixed her hair into two French braids, turned off her light, and went to the kitchen.

Samantha was in the kitchen prepping lunch and snacks for their trip. "Good morning, Laura. It's our first summer shore day, woohoo!"

Laura smiled broadly and moved closer to her mom to help with the peanut butter and jelly sandwiches. The kitchen had brown wooden cabinets and black Formica countertops. The appliances were yellow with black handles. Brown and yellow-flowered wallpaper decorated the walls, and an old rotary phone hung by the wooden kitchen table. Laura opened the freezer and grabbed the ice packs to put into the cooler while Samantha wrapped the sandwiches in tin foil. After Laura and her mom finished putting everything into the cooler, they grabbed the beach bag that was stuffed with towels, sunscreen, and Samantha's *Better Gardening* book.

They headed through the courtyard to the garage. Samantha opened the trunk and threw in the supplies they packed for the day. Laura, looking for the perfect sand toys to take to the beach, rummaged through a corner in the garage before settling on a few buckets, two shovels, and the sand sifter. She threw the items into the trunk, grabbed the beach chairs, and they were off. Laura sat in the front seat with her mom, and they set off to pick up Aunt Penny and Susie. Laura and her mom laughed and talked about the fun they would have. Samantha said, "Penny and I will watch you and Susie swim in the ocean. Too many critters in there for us. We'll enjoy the sunshine and read books."

A few minutes later, they pulled up to the yellow ranch and had barely come to a complete stop when Susie came running down the driveway waving her hands, her smile beaming. Aunt Penny, wearing a large brim sun hat and glasses that swallowed half her face, was carrying their seashore supplies. Everyone took her seat in the car, and they were off. Depending on traffic, the drive to Brigantine was about forty-five minutes.

Samantha and Aunt Penny began singing…

This little light of mine, I'm gonna let it shine. This little light of mine, I'm gonna let it shine. This little light of mine, I'm gonna let it shine, let it shine, let it shine, let it shine.

Laura chimed in.

I won't let Satan blow it out, I'm gonna let it shine. I won't let Satan blow it out, I'm gonna let it shine. I won't let Satan blow it out, I'm gonna let it shine, let it shine, let it shine, let it shine.

They sang more songs and played the alphabet game to pass the time until they finally arrived at the public parking area. The four of them walked across the boardwalk and down the steps to find the perfect place on the sand. Samantha and Penny liked to go to this particular shore for their day trips because it was the closest, and it wasn't usually very crowded.

They found their spot and set up camp. Aunt Penny immediately began digging a hole for her umbrella, while Susie and Laura dropped everything and ran into the ocean. Samantha hollered, "Girls come back here; you didn't even put on any sunscreen, you don't want to burn, come here, please." The girls giggled and splashed water at each other, before running back to Samantha for the sunscreen. Susie and Laura slathered the sunscreen lotion all over from head to toe and wiped their hands on their towels.

"Let's build a sandcastle," Laura said.

The two girls went closer to the water with their buckets and shovels and started digging a moat.

As Samantha and Aunt Penny sat in their chairs, Aunt Penny let out a big sigh and said, "Oh Sammy, the girls are getting so grown up. The time is flying by." Samantha could tell her words were heavier than the typical mom who realizes the days are moving too quickly.

"What's on your mind, Pen?"

Penny began to tell Samantha things were on the rocks with her and Max. "I think he's having an affair," she said. "Max just hasn't been the same. He's drinking a lot more than usual, comes home late at night, and sometimes doesn't come home at all. He had active-duty training just a few weekends ago, and he was mean as a snake when he returned. I don't know what to do. He is my husband until death do us part, right?"

Being the good Catholic she was, Samantha suggested they go to counseling with the priest to try to work things out.

"Marriage is hard sometimes," she said to Penny, "but you have to try everything you can to work it out."

The two women were interrupted by the sounds of giggles drawing closer, "We're hungry. Can we eat lunch?" the girls asked playfully.

Samantha opened the cooler, and everyone took a sandwich and a bottle of water. Sitting in their chairs, they bathed in the sunshine and took in the sites. The sand was brown, which made the water look brown too. Laura didn't mind. She hadn't seen any sand or oceans other than the Jersey shores. The waves crashed, and the water trickled inland along the sand leaving behind a foamy coat mixed with seaweed. On the beach, kids and adults were playing, splashing, and laughing. In Laura's mind, it was the perfect day. She looked to her left, where she could see a beautiful purple and blue butterfly kite flying high in the sky. For a moment, she lost herself as she watched it whiz around beneath the clouds.

"Awww shit," Laura heard, snapping her attention back to the group. Susie was laughing, and Samantha rummaged through her bag as Laura took in the scene around her.

In her daze watching the kite, she didn't notice the seagull that dropped a large poop on her aunt's shoulder.

"Shit, shit, shit," Aunt Penny exclaimed. Everyone was laughing now.

Samantha reached out to help and said, "Shit indeed!" Everyone laughed even harder.

FOUR

October 1986

It had been a while since Laura spent the night at Susie's house. She tried to get her parents to take her on their business trip to Chicago, but they felt it was best she stayed with Aunt Penny. Her parents were looking forward to a well-deserved second honeymoon. Laura hadn't told a single person about her last experience at the yellow ranch. As time passed, she hadn't forgotten what happened, but she did excuse it away in her mind.

Laura helped tidy up in the kitchen after dinner and then she hurried down the hall to Susie's bedroom. Chattering away, Aunt Penny and Susie remained in the living room. The night was cold, and the air stung bitterly with every breath. Susie and Laura had played outside most of the night, and the chill lingered in Laura's lungs. The hope of having a warm shower was on her mind.

Stepping into the darkened room and fumbling for the light switch on the wall, Laura scrambled backward in fright. A burst of lightning revealed an image standing by the doorway. Her heart leaped, and her breathing quickened as Uncle Max stepped through the door and turned on the light located on the righthand side of the wall.

Uncle Max smiled eerily at her, and whispered, "You were searching for the light switch in the wrong place."

Laura did nothing but nod her head as he turned around and walked away. She stood in the doorway and took a moment to catch her breath. The lightning and Uncle Max scared her, but she pushed the thoughts out of her mind.

Entering the bathroom, she slammed the door shut and took care to lock it behind her. She turned the shower knob on to let the water run and get warm. Laura grew comfortable a bit, slipped off her clothes, neatly folded them, and placed them on top of the counter. *BANG,* she heard the storm door slam shut, indicating someone might have stepped out, but she paid little to no attention to it.

The wind outside the house had begun to howl wildly and ram in full force against the rattling windowpanes threatening to give way. The heavens continued to shoot flashes of lightning while the thunderous rumblings accompanied it within seconds as the heavy downpour marched like a thousand boots on the rooftop.

Laura noticed the tiny bathroom was somewhat neat today, mainly because of Susie not having her way with it just yet. Naked and cold and needing a warm shower, Laura stepped into the tub and stood under the gentle spray.

Letting some bouts of water trickle down her spine, she closed her eyes and relaxed her senses with the belief that she was safe behind the locked door. The moment felt warm and glorious. She remained unsuspecting of the figure standing behind her. Uncle Max watched patiently as he slipped off his clothes. Laura gently applied some shampoo to her hair and began massaging her scalp when he made his move.

"Hello, beautiful!" The voice accompanied by the familiar rough and hardened hand called.

Caught off guard, Laura screamed, "Oh my God! Oh my God! Oh my God!" Each one was louder than the previous one.

She screamed at the top of her lungs while he, grinning and smelling of his usual beer stench, sneaked into the shower. Neglecting her screams, he wrapped his arms around her body, confident enough that nothing could come of her yelling as loud as she was.

Laura felt herself threaten to melt and cease to exist as his stiff, nude body pressed against hers from behind. His foul breath continued to contaminate the otherwise sweet-smelling shampooed air she had been enjoying just some seconds before.

"Penny and Susie are out getting some things at the store, so I have you all to myself now," he said in a sickening tone, smirking and extending his reach with each passing second.

Laura kicked hard but found herself powerless as copious thoughts on how to protect herself raced through her mind. None seemed conceivable. She was ten, after all, and the massive body behind her didn't need much to subdue her. He could take whatever disgusting desire his twisted heart craved.

"Please," she heard herself plead. "Please, let me go!"

Her fragile, young frame had begun to shake without console. Max seemed to be taking some thrill from the act of being in power. It was evident by his endless nauseating chuckling while he paused momentarily to subdue her properly, so he could wrap his arms tighter and extend his hand as far as he would like. Laura struggled to breathe, not from lack of air but from the lack of the ability to understand what was going on.

46

Young and baffled, her heart skipped many beats. She prayed in whispers for this invasion to be nothing but a dream, but the reality of the situation made it clear it was not a figment of her imagination. Uncle Max was right there with her, and he wasn't about to leave.

"Ssssshhhh," he placed a finger to his lips and mumbled. "We can both enjoy this if you stop wiggling and crying for help because no one is coming."

Laura nodded, closed her eyes, and felt the warm trickle of tears roll down her cheeks as she clenched her fists together in rage and felt her knees threaten to give way. She sought to remain still and hoped he would leave and bring an end to her torture. However, he only smirked, planted his head atop hers, and held her tightly to his body.

"You've gotten so big and beautiful," he whispered while his left hand reached for her belly button and paused.

Hoping someone would at least hear her and come to her rescue, Laura screamed even louder. "Stop! Please! Please!"

Instead, Uncle Max said, "Fine, scream as loud as you want, little brat, scream and keep screaming. No one is coming, so it doesn't matter. Scream all you want." Laura knew that no one was going to come. And she knew that she couldn't get away.

The badgering sound of raindrops against the rooftop drowned any noise coming from within the house. It was the perfect cover, and the universe seemed to be working with the crazy old man and against Laura that night. She cursed the day underneath her breath. The more she screamed and fought against his touch, the harder he pinned himself around her and threatened to suffocate her.

Laura felt her insides cringe, and her eyes refused to open for fear of witnessing whatever was about to happen. His touch stiffened not just her joints but her soul and her will to breathe as he slowly turned off the shower and began moving his rough hands along her body in gentle trails.

"You like that, don't you?" he asked. "You really like that, don't you?"

The question remained unanswered, but Laura thought to shake her head before gasping in pain and feeling her entire world come crashing down as his hand moved a step farther from her belly button and towards her lower abdomen, further south and towards a region she felt her heart wouldn't be able to manage.

Up until that day, he had always had his clothes on. Of course, she had kept hers on all the time as well, and she learned to be at arm's length, but the devil had other plans set in place with this man.

48

Crouching closely to her ear and whispering, he reminded her one more time, "The longer you resist, the longer this will take."

As terrifying as the words were, Uncle Max was telling the truth. He would, without a doubt, continue to push until he had what he wanted, but she wasn't ready or willing to let him desecrate her innocent body. She would do her best to fight. Laura felt a jolt of adrenalin rush through her veins in one last attempt.

She reached for the blue shower curtain with maps of dirt all over it, yanked at it, and found some support before kicking hard against the wall and hoping he would tumble backward and set her free. The plan was to run as fast as she could. She wasn't going to look back or even try to get her clothes on if she succeeded. His grip only tightened. Determined to get what he wanted, his breath heightened.

Laura finally felt herself break, not on the outside but on the inside. Her stomach felt like it would run out of her mouth, and her throat felt like she was being choked as he pinned himself against her and forcefully held her to the wall. His nude body was pressed against hers now, and Max seemed to want to let her know he had the power. He was in control, and she needed to accept it.

Leaning closer, he said again the exact words she would never come to forget for eternity. "You can scream all you want, my sweet niece, but no one is home, and no one is coming to save you."

Laura felt the shower curtain in her hand slowly slip out of her grasp. She had fought as hard as she could. Her knees felt sore from the number of times she struck them into the wall, and her knuckles felt bruised. He was laughing now, he was so content in his dominance that he rubbed it in her face.

Like a predator finally having its prey by the jugular, he seemed over the moon and elated as he steadied his breath and slowly pulled the helpless little girl to his body. Laura had questions coursing through her mind as she felt his hand reach to the lower part of her abdomen again. She wanted answers as to why someone she cared about and called Uncle Max would commit such a vile act.

This little light of mine... Please, Laura thought, *this little light of mine*, going round and round in her head. She could practically see the light within her getting dimmer. *Satan is blowing it out*, she thought, *I'm gonna let it shine, let it shine, let it shine, let it shine.*

Uncle Max remained oblivious to her and slid his hand down her thigh momentarily before bringing it back up and resting it upon her "lily." Laura felt the sensation trickle down her spine in discomfort. Nothing about the vile act was comfortable, from his rough hands to his heinous crimes.

"Oh yes!" he whispered in satisfaction as he connected with her and stopped momentarily.

Her young, ignorant mind prayed for that to be all. She prayed for it to be all Uncle Max wanted and that he would simply walk away and leave her alone to wash off immediately. The prayer felt like a tall order, but it was what her heart craved and what her soul was crying for at that moment. Laura stood there lifeless, like an empty shell as he proceeded to violate her.

While he brushed his finger along her private area back and forth while making nauseating moans and groan noises behind her, Laura felt sick to her stomach as more tears rushed down her cheeks. Gently moving her hair out of the way and planting his lips on her neck, he tortured her with disgusting kisses. Laura's legs felt weak, and her heart seemed to stop beating. She felt so much shame at that moment. Laura wanted to react, she wanted to beat him, she wanted him to stop, but she felt powerless and had no energy left to fight. Finally, she accepted her fate, stood there, and took it.

Laura's young mind comprehended the thought of death for the first time while she was at the mercy of her sex-deprived Uncle Max. She would rather die than experience another moment. At least that might give her some control.

"I don't want to hurt you," he said, breaking his slimy lips from her neck before planting them back and kissing her again. "I just want to have some fun."

While he continued to rub against her and kiss her neck, Laura felt the prodding feel of something hard against her back. She could feel the jabbing effect his hand made, but she could not comprehend exactly what it was that he was doing. Seconds passed but they felt like hours. Minutes grew into an unending feeling that time was torturing her as she wondered why Susie and Aunt Penny were still not back.

She felt something from behind prod at the opening between her legs when suddenly Uncle Max began to shudder as if he were being electrocuted. She felt a warm stream trickle down her leg, and his coarse lips kissed her neck one more time before he slipped out of the shower, dried himself comfortably, and dressed.

Without uttering a word, he paused and took another lustful look at the little girl, and he sighed in relief before heading out of the room.

Laura was lost, unable to collect any meaning about what just happened. She leaned against the shower wall, her eyes closed tightly as she sang in her head, *this little light of mine, I'm gonna let it shine…*

She cursed the night and the fact that Susie and her Aunt Penny had left her alone with this man. She cursed her presence in the house and why she couldn't have gone with her parents.

Her lips trembled, and every centimeter of her skin felt like it didn't belong to her anymore. Her knees barely held her trembling body upright, and her stomach felt missing while she reached for the hot water knob and slowly began to turn it until she couldn't turn it anymore.

Tightening her grip against the knob, she wished it would go higher and permit more water to rush down on her. She figured the hotter the water, the more it could boil any evil left lingering on her skin.

Why did this happen to me? she thought, as she looked up against the shower as it rushed down her face and body, scalding her as it landed upon her skin.

Hurt, and confused, Laura felt the water hit her sides while she parted her legs and hoped for it to wash off every feel of him from her body. Unfortunately, the feeling was more trapped in her head than in her physical body. Her eyes weighed heavily with floods of tears while she rammed her fists into the wall in frustration.

She wondered what she had done wrong. She couldn't help but feel like she had been bad and brought the sick act upon herself. Uncle Max had violated her, and as little as she knew about adulthood, she recognized his actions to be unjust, wrong, and utterly despicable. Nothing in the mechanics of how his mind worked made any sense to her.

Streams of thoughts began to rush through her mind, thoughts about what her parents would think of her if she told them what had happened.

Will they believe me? What if they assume I have been bad? Would they think I was dirty now, unworthy of love?

As if the feeling of betrayal she felt coursing through her veins wasn't damning enough, the guilt of how her parents might think the worst of her made the awful experience even more complicated. She wished time would stop and as a witness help in telling her pain to her parents. She wished there was some way to let them know everything Uncle Max had done without feeling as guilty as she did right there and then.

Feeling trapped with no answers as to what to do, she turned off the shower and felt the reality of the situation slap her harder. Uncle Max had his way, and there was nobody to protect her. The world felt colder and lonelier as she sobbed profusely and dried herself with hands that trembled.

Finally pulling her clothes back on, she hurried out of the bathroom. Laura didn't want any more of the air that reminded her of everything that just happened. Heading straight for Susie's room, she wondered why the lock to the bathroom had failed her and how he had managed to make his way in. She couldn't help but feel betrayed by everything and everyone and wished her reality would turn out to be a nightmare.

Crawling into bed and folding into a fetal position, Laura felt alone in the world and undeserving to be a part of it for the first time in her life. She closed her eyes and wept aloud while the marching sounds from the heavy downpour slowly diminished against the rooftop. Her own drops of water would continue long into the night, inconsolable and alone with a heavy dose of sadness drowning her heart.

She wasn't ready to stop crying, and she wasn't prepared to step back out until she was sure her cousin and her Aunt Penny were back.

An hour passed, and the storm door slammed loudly and indicated clearly that two people had entered the house by the number of times she had heard it slam back in place. Weak and feeling frail, she slowly got to her feet and dragged herself to the bedroom door. With numerous thoughts racing across her mind, she wondered what would come to be when she finally came across him again.

Should I say something? Laura thought as she walked along the hallway silently.

She didn't want anything to do with him again. But if it were possible to get away from the house at any point, she would run for it without a second thought.

Susie came into view first with a handful of toiletries. "Laura, are you okay?"

Laura stared blankly at her cousin and wondered if she should just let everything out right then. She understood she would be accusing her Uncle Max of a great deal, and her words might not be taken lightly, but she could not ignore the thought of getting some form of revenge and justice over him.

Yet, her heart had lost any strength it had, and she simply nodded her head.

"I'm fine. I fell asleep." The words rolled right off her tongue and embodied the biggest lie she'd ever told.

"Max, are you ready to have your dinner?" Aunt Penny turned to her husband with a smile.

He barely looked away from the TV when he replied, "Sure. Hand me a beer will ya? I'm out."

He didn't seem to notice that Laura walked into the living room. She figured he could tell she was there, but he didn't seem to care at all. Aunt Penny reached for a beer in the fridge and looked around for Susie, but the young girl had gone to the bathroom to put away some items they had purchased from the store.

"Give this to your Uncle Max," Aunt Penny said as she held the beer with an outstretched arm towards Laura.

Bewildered and unsure how to respond, Laura remained stiff momentarily, blinking intermittently while she stared at the cold can of beer still in her Aunt Penny's hand. Aunt Penny stared back at the little girl with a baffled look on her face.

"Yoo-hoo, Laura," she called out, her words startling Laura as she came back into consciousness.

Laura took the beer and slowly turned around with her eyes glued to the ground. She took forever to reach Uncle Max. Finally, unable to find any fitting words, she stretched the can towards him and felt his fingers brush against hers as he snatched his beer, cockily proceeded to open it, and take a sip.

Laura could tell the man bore no emotional turbulence and didn't seem rattled by the events that had occurred prior. She turned around and raced to the kitchen sink in search of soap while her Aunt Penny watched her with worried eyes.

"Can I have some soap, please?" Laura snapped at Aunt Penny without realizing it.

Aunt Penny handed her soap from the kitchen sink, and Laura brushed it against her hands violently as though she had contracted a virus of some kind. After rinsing her hands clean, she began nervously walking away, picking up her pace with each step until she was running back towards her cousin's room.

Susie stood by the door while Laura brushed past and crumbled into the bed in a loud heap. Laura slowly folded into a ball, dragged the blue comforter over her face, and wished she was anywhere but there. She pictured herself being at home and enjoying the safety and comfort of her parents. She missed her parents and her bed. She missed her innocence. She didn't fully understand, but she knew something was forever changed in her that day.

Whimpering in fear and refusing to say a word, Laura couldn't wait for her parents' return. It felt like they had been gone for years, while the events of the previous hour trickled back into her consciousness like it was happening all over again.

She could smell his stench and feel the harshness of his fingers rubbing all over her. She could feel his powerful frame shoving and groping her while her entire world slowly dimmed into one of darkness and pain.

His voice continued to ring in her head like a dreadful and broken silhouette. *"You can scream as loud as you want, my sweet niece, but no one is home, and no one is coming to save you."*

FIVE

Hearing her footsteps hammer hard into the ground while her thumping heart threatened to burst out from her chest, Laura raced out of the house and didn't look back. She had heard the familiar footsteps sneaking her way and had chosen not to go through the same ordeal as before.

Run! Run! were the words drumming in her head and dominating her thoughts as she made the lunge out the storm door.

As always, the door banged her foot, but the pain was nothing compared to what she would feel if "he" caught up with her, so she forged ahead. Racing as fast as her legs would carry her, she tripped over a branch as Uncle Max calmly walked out of the house. Wearing a cynical smile with no mercy across it and his familiar grungy white t-shirt and military-style shorts, Uncle Max pointed in her direction and motioned for her to come here.

Crawling backward on her hands, Laura shook her head and felt the first tear fall as she shouted. "No… please no!"

She wanted nothing more to do with him. She wanted things to be how they used to be, the innocence in her still blooming before a crazed man decided to defile her. She wanted her parents back. All Laura needed was a miracle of some sort, but none seemed to be in sight.

Her Uncle Max took the first step towards the porch smiled, and said, "I will not warn you again."

Watching his disturbing smile slowly morph into an absolutely, terrifying expression, she pulled herself up from the ground, ignored her bruised knee, and hurried down the path tucked in between the bushes just in front of their house. Panting aloud and barely able to catch her breath as she jumped over dead tree trunks, branches, and large stones in her way, she heard nothing behind her and felt she had escaped.

Feeling relieved, Laura stopped, held her breath, and tried hard not to give away her position. She looked back towards the house, which was just a glimmer away. His absence on the front porch brought some discomfort to her heart, but the fact he was nowhere near her came with an unexplainable amount of calm.

"Thank God," the little girl, bruised emotionally, mentally, and physically, breathed in relief, as she sat on a large fallen tree trunk.

Her eyes remained on alert while she looked at the wounds on her knees and hands from her fall earlier. They were bound to heal. Hopefully, scabs would form over them and shed off in time, which wasn't the same thing she could say of her mental state from her awful experience. That was a wound that would undoubtedly take many years to heal. She didn't know it yet, but every ordeal in that house was bound to torment her poor soul for a very long time.

Getting to her feet and trying to limp her way forward with the determination to get as far away from him as possible, she heard a twig snap, paused, and held her breath again. The trees fell dead and bore no sound ahead. She had not noticed it earlier, but no animals seemed to be around. Crickets weren't chirping, birds weren't singing, and no bugs crawled on the ground. Her knees stiffened, and her veins got doused with the feeling of powerful adrenalin pumping through them. Determined to never fall victim again, she turned around and began to jog.

"Laura!" she heard the voice call out before a loud cackle.

She hid behind a large rock and crouched with her head peeking forward and trying to ascertain where he was.

"You are mine!" the vile voice said before she felt his fingers sneak into her hair from behind and grope her.

Uncle Max had circled around and found her. He had good knowledge of the surroundings, and his military training helped him remain unseen. Kicking harder this time around, Laura was determined to put up a fight more superior than the one she had in the bathroom shower. She rammed her legs hard into his knees ignoring how hard he was pulling her hair.

"Leave me alone!" the little girl cried. She kicked and screamed as hard and loud as she could.

"Laura!" a female voice called to her. Laura felt her eyes widen, and the blurry images before her slowly formed into perfection. The trees slowly disappeared, and the soil underneath her bruised knees felt softer now. Her body dripped with sweat; her eyes, face, and neck were wet. The scenery wasn't of the woods any longer, and her heart was suddenly thankful.

"Laura!" the voice belonging to her mom called out once again, and this time with a good degree of clarity.

Laura broke into consciousness and found herself clinging to the back seat of her parents' car. She must have dozed off on the drive home. The bewildered look on Samantha's face matched hers, while they both shared a long stare into each other's eyes.

Having spent the entire night before their arrival without proper sleep, too scared to close her eyes or allow herself to drift off, Laura had finally found some comfort in the backseat. She let herself go for several minutes until her parents decided to wake her when they arrived home.

"You didn't get enough sleep last night, did you?" Samantha asked her daughter. "That's what you get for playing all night with Susie."

That's right I didn't get enough sleep. I was in survival mode at Susie's, Laura thought.

Relaxing a little now that she had finally arrived home, she could attempt to process the heinous events that had taken place.

Laura gently rubbed her eyes and yawned before parting her lips and pausing as she weighed the words she would choose to speak aloud. Thoughts of the shower invasion only sickened her stomach some more while she relived the entire scene in her head again. She briefly considered telling her parents everything but thought it best to sequester herself in her room to think things through first.

Laura finally managed to push out a few words. "I'm tired. I'll be in my room laying down. Can I do my chores later this afternoon?"

Samantha chuckled lightly and said, "Sure. You girls never know when enough is enough. I'd rather you not be cranky all day from lack of sleep. So, yes, please go take a nap, but I'll hold you to those chores. I expect them to get done. Dad and I have to go out back and take care of some yard work. We'll wake you up when we're finished."

Laura retreated to her bedroom and flopped onto her day bed in the far corner by her window. She arranged her pillows so she could sit up in a reclined position while clutching her favorite teddy bear in her hands so she could clear her mind. Laying there rubbing the bear's ears, she stared at her wallpaper, light blue with rows of pink flowers, *pretty carnations*, she thought. Numbly counting the number of flowers on each strip of paper, Laura began to let her mind race. As tears slowly trickled down her face, she began to consider her options. Laura felt ashamed, and the feeling of shame was making it very difficult for her to focus on anything else. She had this burning rage inside, but the anger was directed at herself.

How could I let this happen? How could I not defend myself? Why didn't I tell Aunt Penny the second she got home? Why didn't I demand to leave immediately?

So many thoughts racing through her brain. She tried to remind herself that she was a young girl, and there wasn't much she could have done. Laura knew that she would never be the same and that an adult had taken away her childhood. Now, she had to be the adult. Attempting to reassure herself, she breathed deeply.

Laura allowed her mind to consider telling another adult, someone who could help her sort out her feelings. Her mom or dad was the first logical choice, but she was afraid of this option. Samantha and Paul were devout Catholics, and that good old Catholic guilt is real. She felt unclean, no longer pure, and she didn't feel she could talk about such vile acts. Laura loved her parents. They were wonderful people, but these topics were not discussed in her home. She also thought about her parents' reactions, how the news would bring them so much pain. Laura considered it might be easier for them to deny the vile acts that happened than to face what their daughter had been through, and there was also a small chance they wouldn't believe her.

Clutching the teddy bear even tighter now, her tears had become a steady stream. Her mind continued to race. Perhaps she could tell her 23-year-old sister, Mary. *Mary would understand; she could help*, Laura thought. As she considered this option, she knew that Mary would eventually tell their parents, which wasn't going to be a good plan either. Maybe Matthew, her 24-year-old big brother, could be someone to tell. Suddenly she trembled a little at the thought. *Matthew could never know. He would kill Uncle Max.* For Laura, her older siblings were like having two sets of parents. Matthew was fiercely protective of his sisters, and he didn't always have the most self-control.

Laura had no doubt in her mind that she needed to keep this secret to herself. It was the best thing for everyone. She couldn't break her parents' hearts, she couldn't let her sister carry the burden, and she wouldn't allow her brother to go to jail for murder.

Tossing the bear onto the bed and adjusting her pillows, she lay down to close her eyes. Her innocence was lost and wrapped in an invisible burden.

***

"Dinner's ready," Laura heard her mother call from the kitchen. She had woken previously but didn't feel like facing the day yet and hadn't realized it was dinner time. She sluggishly pulled herself from the bed and stopped by the bathroom to splash some water on her face. She was determined for things to be normal. She dried off her face, picked up the pace, and shimmied into her seat at the kitchen table. Laura was careful to smile and appear upbeat. She didn't want her parents asking any questions.

Dinner lasted for less than thirty minutes, but it felt abnormally long. Samantha and Paul wanted to know all about her stay with Susie. As they ate glazed pork chops, sautéed green zucchini, and yellow summer squash from the garden, they asked Laura if she had a good time with her cousin. That was the first moment Laura learned to feel or think one thing while speaking something different. Intent to keep her secret, she acted as though everything was fine.

Noticing that something seemed to be bothering Laura, Samantha asked, "Did something happen between you and Susie?"

"No, Susie and I are fine. I'm just a little tired. We stayed up playing too late," she simply replied.

Laura got up from the table to hug her parents and started to clear the dishes. She thought busying herself with chores would allow her to avoid answering any more questions from her mom. She didn't know if she would have the strength to contain her emotions, part of her wanted to shout out the truth about what happened right then.

Six

January 1987

Her breath pierced through the silence. Her eyes remained fixated solely on the door before her like it was the gateway to hell. The door stood still, slightly opened to grant her a view of the white-tiled walls just on the other side of it. Laura frozen like a statue, finally moved but barely felt any part of her body go with her.

You can do it, she whispered to herself in the best possible tone of courage she could summon.

It had been three months since that day with Uncle Max, and no part of her own house scared her as much as the bathroom, more specifically the shower. For the younger Laura, it was a place to goof around underneath the water while she would wash clean and even spend some extra minutes singing into the soap as her microphone. Unfortunately, her happy shower memories had been tainted. It had become difficult for her to see the bathroom as a place of comfort and privacy. Evil invaded her shower once before, and Laura couldn't shake the memory. Her paranoia had not been for lack of wanting to get over her fears. However, every time since the awful day with Uncle Max, she was filled with anxiety in the shower. She hoped this time would be different and she could be free from the emotional struggle.

She took a deep breath as she stepped into the bathroom, her mind buzzing unaired words of pain and anguish in remembrance of that most disgusting night.

Being scared had never been her forte, and she had prided her young mind with the ability to be daring, but her experience with Uncle Max was different. It was unspeakable, one that she couldn't fully understand and couldn't share with anyone. That she knew for sure. She hated the feelings of guilt and shame and wished she could rid herself of them.

She wanted to fight, face her demons head-on rather than hide away or shy away from them. She didn't understand the emotions she felt. They were heavy like luggage strapped to her back. She wanted to move on and just be a kid.

One day at a time, she thought…*one day at a time, I will get through this*. Laura willed herself to move forward as she had done every day since her body was violated. *He is not here. He won't hurt you*, she whispered to herself as she tried to remain calm. With another deep sigh and the determination swelling in her heart, she pushed forward and took the first step towards the mirror hanging above the bathroom sink to regale herself with a shattered image reflecting sadness back at her. Unfortunately, it wasn't the same. Nothing about Laura's face staring back at her seemed likable. It lacked the wild and widened smiles across her face each time she investigated the mirror in the past. Certain things were missing. The happy-go-lucky little girl who stared back at her just several months ago was gone.

The reflection felt stained, and with it came a saddened reflection of pain and hollowness that could not be measured.

This is your bathroom, she repeated in her head. *You are in YOUR bathroom, you are safe.*

Laura wanted this simple task to be easy again. She wanted nothing more than control over the situation. Closing her eyes while she gently pulled her shirt over her head, her stomach felt a slight tingle of worry mixed with fear, but she needed to move past that now. *It happened, it's over, and you need to move on,* she told herself again and again.

She finished undressing, picked up her clothes, and dropped them into the laundry basket, which was already full to the brim—one of her undone chores. Her day-to-day was unquestionably in a hellish state, and she needed it to stop. She wanted her life back, the one she had before he defiled her. She wanted the joy of being a child to come back, the safety and innocence that childhood brought.

Laura took the first bold step forward. Her heart skipped a beat momentarily. Finally, underneath the running water, her heart resumed its drumbeat, but her mouth soured with tastes from the displeasing memories. Laura had not realized it yet, but it wasn't her presence in the shower that continued to trouble her; it was the endless questions she had continued to ask of herself, questions that centered around the disgust, pain, and betrayal she still felt swirling inside. The feelings were burning from the inside out, and each day, she hoped for strength to overcome her shame and horrible memories of his touch, his voice, and his horrible actions.

She felt trapped as if her predator's memory continued to eat away at her purity. It contaminated every ounce of her life. All she had left was this indescribable feeling of being corrupted, and she couldn't figure out why she deserved it.

She could see him grinning through the reflective surfaces of each tile. She shut her eyes and prayed for more strength. Yet, her mind continued to replay the scene in her head over and over. Her feet threatened to slide off the floor as if they didn't want anything to do with holding her up any longer.

Every shower since that awful night brought nothing but deep and horrendous flashbacks, flooding through her mind. She felt so alone. She felt cold loneliness inside, but she was getting better at concealing her feelings on the outside. Externally, she had moved on, and no one was the wiser. She went to school, did her homework, helped with the garden, and collected chicken eggs each morning. She wore her smile every day like it was an accessory.

She reached for the shower knob and felt her grip stiffen around it momentarily. Then, beads of tears too cold to bear slowly began rolling down her cheeks and onto her lips, causing them to tremble. Finally, silent cries in the shower allowed some of what she was feeling inside to escape.

Why me? she asked herself for the umpteenth time. *Why did he do this to me?*

The bold questions continued while her hand slowly reached for the shower knob once again and she turned it a little more.

Did I do something wrong?

With every question asked, she had the underlying feeling that she indeed did nothing wrong. With her grip tightened firmly around the knob, she turned it all the way up. Laura felt herself move from the point of feeling sorry for herself to wanting to know what she had done wrong. She felt herself transition from cowering in fear to demanding answers to her questions.

Hearing herself mumble the questions subtly but sternly brought some air of relief to her as she slowly felt the shower water reach the hottest point. She always needed to have the water as hot as possible. It seemed to be exactly what her skin needed. The soothing feeling the boiling water brought her skin was impossible to explain, but it burned away the torment that continued to linger on her flesh. She wanted more. She wanted the ability to walk into her bathroom, step under the shower, and let it rush down without an atom of anxiety in her heart.

Her parents always taught her to be strong, and she knew that she was. As much as she was struggling now, she knew she would overcome his evil deeds. She would let her light shine.

"You're wrong," she finally muttered with as much conviction as she could muster. "You're at fault, you asshole. Not me!"

It would be the first time she acknowledged that out loud. Standing there she let the water run down her hair and into her face in a mixture of joy and sadness, all curled into one. She smiled for the first time in months and felt her face sincerely glow in warmth as the shower continued to stream down onto her. It felt perfect and safe, which were the two things she missed the most in her life.

Reaching for the shampoo, she applied some to her hair and rubbed it into her scalp. Laura had just placed her head under the shower to rinse and suddenly she halted. The air grew colder, and the hair on the back of her neck stood up. Her hands began to tremble while she stared at them, and the floor seemed to slowly rotate, bringing her focus into a rather hazy view as she struggled to find her balance. She wasn't sure of what was going on until she realized a trail of shampoo had streamed down her shoulder and onto her back. Another flashback she had no control over, it was another stark reminder of the unforgettable memory.

Laura hoped to scream but had no strength to get it out. Her voice box felt stuffed, and the hissing sound from the running water mimicked his demand for her to remain silent when he placed a finger to his lips and warned her.

Feeling her world slowly begin to unravel again right before her eyes, Laura cried, "Oh my God!"

Her young mind was battered. She was foolish to think that she had overcome her emotional triggers so quickly. Uncle Max had scarred her in varying ways, and every single one of them needed healing, endless amounts of healing.

Each drop of water felt like a thousand needles wrapped in one, poking at her back. The water running down her spine felt as harsh as his hands when he ran them across her skin. She wanted more of the pain from the hot water in hopes it would finally burn everything away and leave her with nothing tying her memories to him.

Leave me alone! she raged inside. *Leave me... leave me... leave me alone and go away!*

SEVEN

Summer 1987

The day was Saturday and Laura woke early, at 7:00 a.m. to be exact. She needed to help her mom, so Laura grabbed the little brown basket that hung outside on the back patio and skipped outside to greet the chickens. The coop had an inside and outside portion, all covered by the same black shingle roof. Laura used to call it the chicken house and the back porch. She imagined the chicks would sleep inside and hang out for some girl time on the porch. The house was a six by six-foot space with twelve little cubby stalls, one for each chicken. Laura undid the latch to enter the house. Her job was to check the stalls for eggs. Delighted, she carefully placed six fresh brown eggs into her basket. Nothing tasted better than fresh eggs from the coop. She liked to visit with the chickens in the morning. They were Rhode Island Reds with feathers that ranged from deep pink to almost black. The mixture of colors made the chicks look mostly brown. They had bright red earlobes, and wattles, and their eyes were red-orange. Laura felt like they could look right at her, and they would understand everything she was saying.

"Good morning chick-a-dees," she sang, "How are my little chicks today?"

She could see the trough was already full of food, so her dad must have come out and fed them. Laura was proud of the red chicken coop, which she helped her daddy build. She was even more proud of the chickens. Laura thought it was unique to have animals in the backyard that could produce eggs that her family actually ate.

She knew her mom would soon be calling for her, so she quickly checked all the doors one more time, making sure they were fastened tightly before heading back toward the house. Opening the glass sliding door with one hand and the egg basket in the other, she called to her mom, "Mom, we have six eggs today!"

Samantha said, "Oh, the girls are getting older now and aren't laying as much. Your dad and I have talked to Princeton Lavender about getting some new ones."

Confused, Laura asked, "What do you mean, new ones? Will we get more chickens? We already have twelve, and the coop can't hold more than twelve."

Trying to avoid the topic of slaughtering the chickens with her daughter, Samantha said, "Come on now. We need to get to work. Put the eggs into the fridge and wash up your hands. There's an apron on the chair for you to wear."

The apron was black with a cursive script that said Princess of the Kitchen with a crown titled over the P. Laura grabbed the apron and put it on. She loved spending time cooking with her mom. Her favorite day to cook was Sunday, because her mother made linguini noodles, tomato sauce, meatballs, and bread from scratch. Samantha wasn't Italian, but Paul was. His parents immigrated to the US from Sicily. Samantha used to joke that it was a condition of their marriage that she learned to cook Italian like Granny Shirk!

Samantha was a beautiful woman. Standing 5 feet 7 inches tall, her long wavy hair was dark brown, almost black, tied up in a bun. She was not a slender woman but rather fit with some curves. Samantha was leaning over the counter and reading a cookbook. A large stockpot was on the yellow stove, and canning jars were spread out on the black Formica countertop. Sitting next to the cookbook was a large basket of peaches.

Samantha said, "Your dad and I picked these yesterday. We are going to can them so we can save them for later."

Laura had not canned peaches before, but she had helped her mom can other things. They canned tomatoes and pickles and homemade strawberry jam, all picked fresh from the garden.

Her mother instructed her to pick up the peeling knife, for Laura's job was to wash and peel the peaches while Samantha sliced them. They worked together for hours, finally stopping for lunch. Samantha made some turkey sandwiches, and the two sat at the kitchen table. They enjoyed some lemonade and rested for a few minutes.

"Laura, your dad and I are going to take a trip. We are going on a pilgrimage to Medjugorje for ten days."

Medjugorje was a small village in Yugoslavia, presently known as Bosnia-Hercegovina.

"The Blessed Virgin Mary has been appearing and giving messages to the world," Samantha said. "The Blessed Mother says she's come to tell the world that God exists. He is the fullness of life, and to enjoy this fullness and peace, you must return to God," she continued.

Samantha explained that a very good friend was critically ill, and they were going together on a spiritual journey to see the visionaries: Ivan, Jakov, Marija, Mirjana, Vicka, and Ivanka. The blessed mother appeared before them and shared her message with the visionaries so they could share it with the world.

Medjugorje was a holy land that brought strength and renewed spirit.

Samantha said, "We leave in a few weeks. I have arranged for you to stay with Aunt Penny."

Laura's stomach sank. She had just barely started to put the whole incident behind her, and now she was expected to stay with them for ten entire days. She sat in silence eating her lunch as her mother droned on about the details. Laura had retreated to the far corners of her mind, her mother's voice a fog in the distance.

Samantha said, "Laura, Laura…hello little girl! Are you listening to me?"

"Sorry, Mom, I was daydreaming. Got it, Aunt Penny's for ten days." Laura said, without feeling.

"Yes, you and Susie will have a great time. Now come over here and help me with these peaches. They aren't going to finish canning themselves." Samantha said with a smile.

EIGHT

Everything about the picture felt wrong, everything from the dirt-ridden ground with overgrown and unkempt grass to the foul air that unsettled every corner of her stomach and lungs. She had fought against going to Aunt Penny's as best she could. From the instant, the information shattered her ears, she tried every means possible not to have to go there again.

"I don't want you staying with your brother or sister for this long!" Samantha said angrily after hearing Laura protest several times.

It was late Summer. School would start in a few weeks, and she had hoped the day would involve her spending time with her parents. Laura played the sick card, but none of her schemes seemed to work. They only enraged Samantha who demanded Laura get herself into the car immediately. Paul had also made compelling arguments why Laura needed to be at her cousin Susie's. Laura couldn't blame her parents; they didn't know. She kept her secret hidden deep down so no one would know. It had been several months since her last visit to Susie's, but there she was again, standing on the front porch and feeling sorry for the barking beagle. She could relate to him, chained up with no place to go. He too seemed like he was concealing secrets he wanted to express. Her heart broke for him being tied to that chain all day. Waving as her parents' car drove away, Laura was uncomfortable as she wondered how she would survive the next ten days.

Her legs refused to move.

"Susie is waiting for you in the backyard, honey," her Aunt Penny shouted from the living room window.

The fact remained that Laura couldn't come to terms with staying at the evil home another night. She couldn't swallow the thought of it, but she had to, especially with Susie now rushing through the door and coming to hug her excitedly.

Still unsure of what the reality of things would be, Laura entered the house as the storm door slammed shut and slowly reminded herself of just how many entities could hurt her within the house.

Scared stiff and afraid to look towards the living room, she slowly walked ahead where the sound from the TV meant Uncle Max was there watching *M.A.S.H* or some other show. Laura stopped upon hearing her name.

"Laura!" her Uncle Max called out in a cheery tone. "It's good to have you over after such a *long* time. Come and hug your Uncle Max!"

Fortunately, he seemed composed, much unlike his usual touchy self. He patted Laura on the shoulder. His touch brought back her pain and shame. Laura wiggled out from his grasp as soon as possible. She moved her bags from the front door into the living room and followed Susie through the kitchen and outside to the backyard.

Laura's plan was simple. She would stick with her Aunt Penny wherever the lady went and never leave her side. She hoped her aunt could keep her safe until her parents returned to take her home.

The morning felt normal for the time being, and she prayed the normalcy lasted until the very end. She would count the days one by one.

***

As the day went by, all Laura could think about was the horror of stepping back inside the house. Surprisingly, Uncle Max had made no appearance and allowed the day to run smoothly. Laura couldn't help but be on edge the first few hours after her arrival.

Laura wondered if Susie could be trusted with the secret of Uncle Max's horrific deeds. She thought about telling her on numerous occasions but held back. Laura was sure Susie wouldn't handle the information well.

"It's getting dark," Susie said with a scowl as they packed up the balls and the blanket Aunt Penny had brought outside.

"Susie…?" Laura started to say.

Susie looked at Laura with a deep and sad stare before racing over to hug her. Laura could sense that something was bothering her, but she too, could not share.

Like kindred spirits too scared to voice what troubled their young souls, the duo remained in each other's embrace. As Aunt Penny opened the backdoor to walk out of the house, she stared at the girls. Smiling, she waved for them to get back inside.

Laura could have sworn she heard Susie use a swear word or two, but the young girl had been wise enough not to speak them too loudly. Laura could feel something wasn't right. Something about Susie's demeanor had been bothersome whenever they talked about having to go inside. They played outside all day.

"Can I help in the kitchen?" Susie asked as she walked past her mother.

"Of course, honey," Aunt Penny replied.

Susie's face lit with jubilation. Laura's face filled with desperation to be included in whatever task they were starting.

Reaching for Laura and gently laying her hand to rest on the girl's head, Aunt Penny smiled and whispered, "You can join us in the kitchen too, dear. Please go wash your hands first."

"Laura, you're at the sink so you stay there on dish duty, and Susie will handle the knife and do the cutting," Aunt Penny said before disappearing.

Susie looked towards the living room where her father continued to drown himself in beer, as evident by the five empty bottles perched at the foot of the couch a short distance from his legs. They watched him yawn and sip some more from the half-empty bottle in his hand. He surfed the channels to find something that suited him.

Laura took comfort that Susie would be around the entire time. Thoughts churned in Laura's mind. She wanted to give her Uncle Max the benefit of the doubt. Maybe he was confused or simply not in control of his mind when he proceeded to act in the terrible way he had several months ago. Maybe, just maybe, it would never happen again.

***

If only Laura had woken up to hear her Aunt Penny calling out for Susie to get in the car that morning. Her night's rest was decent, she slept with her back to the wall, curled up with her pillow to her chest.

Noticing she was by herself, Laura let out a yawn, rubbed her eyes with both hands, and stared around the room. Her heart practically stopped beating, and then it started to beat like a drum in a parade.

What's going on? Where's Susie? Laura thought while sitting up and stretching until the comforter draped across her chest fell to the ground.

Laura thought that maybe Susie was in the bathroom, but she didn't dare get out of bed and check. Her lower jaw unhinged while she thought about shouting for Susie and praying that she *was* in the bathroom.

Laura looked to the door immediately and felt herself curl from the inside out. She took a deep breath and swallowed hard while she hoped her worst fears wouldn't emerge.

Stay in the room and don't go out, she thought to herself before grabbing hold of the comforter from the floor.

Leaving the room for any reason wasn't going to be an option for Laura. She figured she would shelter herself in the protection of remaining in the room. If she were alone while her Aunt Penny and Susie were out, it increased the possibility that Uncle Max would try to mess with her.

Closing her eyes with her head gently resting atop the pillow, she slowly began to relax. Laura, assuming she was sheltered in safety, felt she was going to be okay. *Surely he couldn't violate me again*, she thought.

It began when the door slowly opened, followed by the large, old-looking sandals and black socks coming into view before the familiar sight of the green military khaki and grungy white undershirt. She didn't want to look up, but his heinous face wasn't hard to miss with the smirk of mischief beaming across it.

Placing a finger to his lips as he neared the bed, Uncle Max looked back towards the bathroom, but he didn't seem to care much. Laura hoped with her entire being that there was someone in there. The air in the room thinned immediately, and her lungs felt like they had collapsed. She reached for the comforter and tightened her grip as she prayed it was nothing but a terrible dream.

"Please!" Laura whispered without realizing the words had come out.

A part of her had hoped he still bore a conscience. She wanted to beg him not to hurt her again. Praying for his conscience felt like the only weapon she had. Her joints froze when he crawled into bed like a snake from the pits of betrayal.

"Be a good little girl for me now, and I promise this will be over before you know it," he whispered.

Laura, hoping she might be able to spring out of bed and run away, looked towards the open bedroom door. Unfortunately, he seemed to read her thoughts and grabbed for her wrist, which he bound tightly in his rough hand.

"You wouldn't want me to hurt you now, would you?" he said as he used his other hand to cover her mouth.

Perceiving the words of truth from his stench-ridden mouth, she nodded her head in response as her eyes bulged with fear.

"Just lay down there and help your Uncle Max feel really good," he snickered.

Laura felt her voice collapse and her entire body shudder with nothing short of shame. She was trapped again. Lying still while beads of hot tears rolled from her eyes, she wished her consciousness would drift away, and her body would be nothing but a shell as the man desecrated it without mercy or respect.

"That's my good girl... that's my good girl," he mumbled with his lips scraping away at her tender skin and making sure he scarred her for life even if the scars wouldn't show externally.

Helpless and unable to hold back how she felt, Laura let out the first muffled scream that brought him to a stop as he knelt over her and scowled.

"They cannot save you," he warned. "They just left. It's just you and me, kid."

Releasing his hand from her mouth and assuming a more comfortable position over her while he knelt, he reached for the center of his pants. He began massaging the region with his eyes closed and his breath quickening. Laura let out a louder scream in hopes that anyone would hear, but he moved fast, clamping his hand over her mouth again and shooting her a repulsive glare.

Laura swore to herself she wouldn't be helpless this time, she wouldn't let him have his way without a fight. Regardless of how weak she looked or powerless she knew she was, she chose to fight back. Pushing him backward she attempted to get his stinking frame off her. Uncle Max grumbled at her angrily before grabbing for her hands and pinning them down hard above her head.

"You're hurting me!" Laura pleaded while his fingers dug into her wrists and scratched her tender skin.

Uncle Max, ignoring her plea, smiled happily as he pressed his burly shape over her. She could feel his chest touching hers through her shirt. Laura struggled for air and whimpered as his unbearable stench threatened to knock her unconscious. She kicked hard, but he continued to subdue her by holding her hands together tightly and slamming them into the wooden headboard.

"Why haven't you learned? It will feel better if you stop fighting," he whispered into her ear with his stinky breath.

Laura shook her head before tasting the horrifying feeling of hopelessness trapped inside every drop of her tears as they landed on her lips.

"You're hurting me, and I don't want any of this. Why don't you listen?!" She said with every ounce of strength she could muster. *Why haven't I learned, why don't YOU listen, why are you doing this?* She thought.

Laura wiggled to no avail and felt her freedom snuffed from her entire body by the man she wanted to believe was her uncle and should be protecting her.

"You look so ripe, so young and so beautiful," he whispered.

"Stop, Uncle Max!" she begged fervently and felt her tears get even thicker as they flowed down her cheeks.

He placed his hand on her mouth once more to prevent her from speaking any further.

"You aren't enjoying it because you keep struggling!" he said before taking his hand off the center of his pants and hovering it over her face and acting as though he was going to strike her cheek.

Laura feared the worst was about to come from him, and her skin began to crawl. The hairs on the back of her neck froze in an upright position, and her eyes slammed shut as no part of her wanted to see the man defile her once again.

Laura continued to sing in her head…

This little light of mine…

Don't let Satan blow it out…

Let is shine, let it shine, let it Shine…

Uncle Max reached for her shirt with his right hand, sneaking it underneath and feeling her belly button before moving north and landing his rough fingers upon her nipple. He fondled her chest and felt the girl continue to squirm. He then proceeded south and towards her pants while Laura struggled fervently and tried to roll him over.

"Please just stop… Uncle…Uncle Max. I will do anything you want but just STOP!" she cried amidst the endless river of tears burning down her cheeks.

His strength prevailed, and he managed to pin her hands even tighter while he snaked the other hand down her pants and shot her a depraved look that would remain etched in her memory for life. He flicked his disgusting finger back and forth along her vagina before he finally settled just inside her. Laura looked toward the door with teary eyes. She prayed and cried, *this little light of mine* still played in her head on repeat. Her eyes stayed focused on the door while her mind stayed focused on the song. She went somewhere else. She didn't know where, but she was no longer present at that moment.

Eventually, Uncle Max crawled away from her without a word, adjusted his clothes, and headed out of the room. Laura remained frozen, too grief-stricken to speak, too sore all over. Her skin felt like it didn't belong to her anymore. Her entire body felt devoid of life and the will to live. She wished she could exchange it for her innocence once again at any cost.

Jumping out of bed, Laura packed and ran from the room. Her wrists remained sore, and she could still feel him pinning her into the bed.

I want to leave, she begged to herself with swollen and reddened eyes as she sniffed and wiped tears from her cheeks.

She arrived in the living room, and there he sat like it was any other day. No big deal, nothing happened here. He sat nonchalantly, as though he didn't just violate his niece in his daughter's bedroom a few steps away. He gulped his beer as always and watched his TV without even looking her way.

Aunt Penny and Susie returned shortly after.

"I want to go home," Laura demanded rather than asked.

"Are you okay, honey? Your eyes are red," Aunt Penny said as she drew closer and placed her hand on Laura's shoulder.

Laura shook her head. "I want my mom and dad, and I want to go home, now!"

She said nothing further; she wanted to go home, and that was all that mattered.

NINE

Silence as a noun means a complete absence of sound. Silence as a verb means to prohibit or prevent speaking. Laura had become very familiar with both meanings of silence.

Laura and Susie were playing Scrabble at the kitchen table and Laura was winning. Susie had the fancy version of Scrabble with the plastic spaces that held the pieces in place. It was Susie's turn, and she was biting her lip as she considered what word she would make next. She needed 25 points to catch Laura, and she wasn't going to give up without a fight!

Bam Bam Bam Bam

Bam Bam Bam Bam Bam Bam

Susie jumped from the table to the edge of the kitchen and peered around the corner. Confused, Laura looked at her.

Holding a finger to her lips, Susie motioned for Laura to come next to her. Both girls peeked around the corner now and could see shoes flying through the bedroom door and slamming against the wall in the hallway.

Suddenly, *BAM*, a black military boot flew against the wall and created a large hole. The voices were getting louder and louder, as they yelled and screamed.

"You are an asshole, Max! I know you've been sleeping with Jeanne. I saw her! I saw her with you weeks ago. I saw your car at that cheap motel. You fucking bastard. You sit around here drunk half the time. I can't take it anymore." Aunt Penny raged through tears as she continued yelling wildly and throwing things at him. "Coming in all hours of the night, vomiting in the toilet. You don't love anything but your dick and your booze."

"You're a bitch, Penny," Uncle Max shouts back. "A man needs what a man needs, and you just don't give it to me. You don't *DO IT* for me anymore. You've lost your mind. I am the man of this house." Uncle Max screamed. "I will do as I please."

Aunt Penny was grunting now, "Max, you aren't a man. You're a drunk! GET OUT, GET THE FUCK OUT OF THIS HOUSE RIGHT NOW!"

Susie and Laura scurried back to their seats and pretended to go back to their Scrabble game. Uncle Max came storming down the hallway with his giant green military duffle bag hoisted over his shoulder. As he entered the living room, he dropped the bag onto the floor.

Aunt Penny's crying could be heard faintly from the kitchen. Uncle Max came into the room to hug Susie. "I love you, Susie. You are always my best girl. I will be back in a few days. I need to go to duty training at Fort Dix," he lied as he patted her head, picked up his bag, and walked out the door.

Devastated, Susie said, "This has been going on for a while. Mom and Dad have been fighting a lot. Mom says he drinks too much."

Laura could tell that Susie was hurting, and she wanted to be there for her, but Laura could hardly contain her relief that Uncle Max was gone. Maybe now the rest of her days would be safe.

"Let's go outside and play," Susie said. She wanted to be out of the house and didn't want to see or hear her mom upset. She loved both of her parents and didn't understand why they fought.

Trying to help, Laura said, "Sure, let's go make mud-pies down the street!"

The girls put all the Scrabble letters back into the black velvet bag, folded the board, and neatly placed everything back in the box.

Susie put the game back in her room as she hollered to let her mom know they were going to Old Man Wister's place down the block.

Old Man Wister's was on the corner next to a large field. All the kids on the street liked to go down there and play, especially to make mud-pies.

Laura and Susie headed toward the old two-story brick house and kicked rocks along the road as they walked. Susie was glad to be outside and away from the chaos.

Standing alone in the middle of a big field, Old Man Wister's house looked almost haunted. Leading from the road to the entryway was a long winding gravel driveway. Standing tall next to the house was a single lonely tree, a dogwood. Moss had taken root along the base of the little old house.

Old Man Wister was outside working in his garden. He waved, and Laura and Susie smiled. He was a nice old man, but he kept mostly to himself. A crow sat atop the black pointy roof, and the windows seemed to be watching the street.

Laura imagined hidden stories inside the walls of the old house. She could relate, for she had gotten very good at hiding her feelings. What choice did she have? Some things were best to continue in silence. For her, it was life's unwanted experiences; for the house, it was tales from the inside.

At the corner of the road was an old, abandoned lot. Several wooden pallets leaned upright against a rusty old Chevy. The rain the night before had left the ground wet and muddy. Cinder blocks were stacked up in a zigzag pattern. It was like a hidden junkyard or perhaps a treasure trove of fun, depending on how you looked at it. The girls loved to play hide and seek, make mud-pies, tell stories, and let their imaginations run wild. They could be anyone in this place.

Squish, squish, squish, the mud dribbled through their fingers. Susie squished her mud-pie into a little round ball. She set the ball on top of a cinder block to adorn it with blades of grass and one little purple flower she found by the road.

The girls laughed and played and made a feast of mud-pies. Laura wished that she could be home, but for a moment, everything seemed like it would be ok.

Later that evening, Aunt Penny ordered pizza. They watched the movie *Beaches*, as they snuggled with cozy blankets in the living room, the three of them had a girls' night.

"I know you miss your parents, sweetie, but they are halfway across the world, and they aren't able to come and get you. We will have fun this week, I promise,"

Aunt Penny said to Laura in an assuring tone. Everyone seemed at least a little relieved that Uncle Max was gone.

As they watched the movie, Laura let her mind wander. She knew she wouldn't be able to talk to her parents this week. They were too far away and international phone calls were expensive. She didn't even know what time it was where they were.

Instead, she imagined she was snuggled up with her favorite blanket at home and nestled in the safety of her mother's and father's arms.

TEN

S amantha said, "I hope Laura is okay. She seemed pretty upset when we left her at Penny's."

"She'll be fine," Paul tried to reassure his wife.

"And that Max! I don't know what Penny's going to do about him. She told me a lot when we were at the shore. He doesn't treat her very well." Samantha and Paul exchanged a worried look and continued talking until their train pulled into the station.

Arriving in Dubrovnik, they collected their luggage, awaiting instructions from the guide. Luka, their tour guide had arranged for all of them to stow their bags at a local hotel so they could sightsee and spend the day taking in the city.

The group had several hours before they would depart on their nearly three-hour bus journey to Medjugorje. Luka directed everyone to the hotel and assisted with arrangements for their belongings. He was local, funny, and friendly.

"You can do whatever you like, cause a little trouble, but maybe not too much." Luka laughed. "I can assist you if you have questions, need directions, or suggestions. But, most importantly, be back here at 5 p.m. to catch the bus. Don't be late. We will leave without you," he said with a thick Croatian accent.

The city was simple but beautiful. The hills rolled right along the coast. Houses and buildings with brown clay roofs filled the town. Samantha, of course, had planned everything each day for them and purchased cassette tapes to learn Croatian before the trip.

She walked over to Luka to get a second opinion on their itinerary while Paul took in the sites around him. Upon her return, they were off to grab something to eat. They walked a little way down the cobblestone streets to a restaurant called Pantarul. Nestled in the Old Town, the little family-run restaurant served a variety of local dishes.

As they ate, Samantha brought up Laura again and hoped that she was having a good time.

"She is in good hands, and the girls will have a blast together." Paul said, "I bet she won't even want to come home when we get back."

Samantha knew that everything would be fine, but she missed her little girl.

The couple sat eating their lunch and discussing the details of their trip. They had planned to stay with a local host family in Medjugorje, similar to a bed and breakfast. In the morning, Samantha and Paul planned to attend church at St. James.

St. James Parish Church was a beautiful white building with two tall towers, one on each side covered in floor-to-ceiling square windows with blue triangle peeks at the top. Atop each peek stood a tall metal cross. After church, they would listen to the visionaries speak and share the Blessed Mother's message.

"I'm looking forward to going to church," Paul said, "but when do we climb Mount Krizevac?"

"The plan is to climb the mountain on Wednesday," Samantha replied.

The cross on Mt. Krizevac overlooked the village of Medjugorje. Krizevac meant "Mount of the Cross." The mountain was also known as Cross Mountain. Built in 1933, a 16-ton cross stood at the summit. Climbing the mountain was part of the pilgrimage. Samantha didn't like climbing or heights, but Paul was looking forward to this part of their journey.

"We'll have a wonderful time in prayer, bringing us closer to God. This will be a wonderful trip." Paul said. "And Laura will have a great time at home," he assured his wife again.

ELEVEN

Only two days left to go before she could greet her parents from their trip. Since Uncle Max left, things had been fun at Susie's. Laura had done her best to make the most of her time with her Aunt Penny and Susie. They baked cakes, played cards, watched movies, and painted each other's nails.

Laura had woken up early in the morning and went to the kitchen to get some water. Already awake, Aunt Penny was sitting at the kitchen table and reading the latest *Glamour* magazine. Suddenly, the storm door creaked open and slammed back on its frame.

From the moment of his arrival, she sat staring at the wall clock, watching exactly five minutes tick by. Laura had wondered if there was some cosmic pull bringing her back to the Bermuda Triangle of her emotions. Laura had held her breath and only forced herself to speak when her Uncle Max greeted her.

"Morning," she had simply replied in a tone empty of any hint that she was interested in speaking to him. She hoped her body language would help give off the vibe. Laura squirmed as her heart raced out of control and she wondered if she was about to have a heart attack. It would be fitting given the current situation, even if she was too young. Her fingers gripped tightly onto the underside of her chair, and her nails dug into the wood nervously. Making sure she was still taking in air, she paid careful attention to her breath.

She wanted to leave; she wanted out of the house. She wanted to be as far away from him as possible. With Uncle Max in the house, the air felt toxic, both literarily and figuratively, and her eyes grew sore as she feared to blink.

"Oh my God!" she whispered and gasped before noticing her Aunt Penny had been staring at her for a while.

Aunt Penny leaned closer and asked, "Are you okay, darling?"

Laura feigned a smile and replied, "Yes, Aunt Penny. Should I wake Susie up?"

"Yes, go ahead and wake her. Let her know her father's home," Penny quietly said.

Laura nodded but remained seated. From Aunt Penny's gaze, she could tell that the lady wondered why she hadn't moved to wake her cousin in the bedroom.

Laura knew why and wished the woman knew half as much as she did, maybe that way, things could be different. The thought of Aunt Penny finding out how much of a demon her husband was rippled through Laura's mind. But who was Laura to tell her? She parted her lips in hopes of giving Aunt Penny a hint but halted as the air in the room suddenly felt even dirtier. It felt thick with betrayal, worry, and dreadfulness all wrapped into one ball of disturbing emotion. Looking like the green snake he was, Uncle Max had just waltzed his way unconcerned through the front door and into the living room.

You fucking bastard! Laura thought to herself and wished she could voice the words aloud. Those were harsh words for someone her age, but Laura didn't care. She felt they fit the situation perfectly.

She watched him draw closer, wearing his characteristic shorts and t-shirt. He stopped just a few feet from her. Laura could still smell his stench. The stench her young mind told her was everything wrong in a man.

As Laura left the room, she had to strain to hear Aunt Penny's words. "Max, I know we discussed you coming home and trying to work things out, but I didn't realize you would be home this soon."

Uncle Max, speaking gently, raised his hands and tilted his head at Aunt Penny as he began to saunter towards her. He said, "Oh Pen, I've missed you and

Susie. I know I need to do better, but you still love me, right? I was ready to come home, so I came home. How about you fix me some eggs?"

"It's good to have you back, but we do have some things we need to work on." Then she smiled and said, "Susie should be out here in a minute. She'll be happy to see you."

Susie was sound asleep under the covers when Laura entered the room. She decided to sit on the bed a minute before waking her cousin. Laura sat staring at the wall and noticed a few cobwebs in the corner sparkling just right in the light.

She rocked her cousin gently and said, "Susie, you need to wake up. Susie, Suuuuuu-siiiiieeeee." Laura could feel the terror of the next two days filling up inside of her. She had to survive two days with him in the house, two whole days. Speaking a little louder now, "Susie, your dad's home. GET UP!"

Susie's eyes shot open as she leaped up and ran to the kitchen as Laura followed slowly behind her. Susie plopped down at the table next to her dad, her eyes were beaming into his.

Smiling, he said to Laura, "Come sit with us and eat some eggs."

Laura declined by shaking her head fervently. "No thank you, I'm not hungry."

"Sure, you are, come sit!" Uncle Max exclaimed.

She turned around and headed toward the living room.

"Is something wrong?" Susie asked as Laura began to walk away.

Laura replied, "I'm fine."

Laura wished she could out the man for who he was, a wretched monster and pedophile.

***

The first half of the day felt like a win considering things had gone rather smoothly. Laura had managed to summon the courage to play inside the house later in the afternoon. However, her mind didn't forget about the evils that could come to befall her at any point in time.

Having been subjected to the lowest level of human indecency by a man, Laura had grown in ways she could not explain. Her senses had taken on heightened states that subconsciously caused her to listen for incoming footsteps, breathing, or other sounds.

He will not show up, Laura said to herself while Susie sorted the Legos out. *I am safe.*

Unfortunately, that wasn't the case, for the door swung open aggressively, and Uncle Max stood in the doorway. He was angry and displeased. His eyes bulged from their sockets as though he was about to implode, and his fist tightened in clench around the doorknob as he tried to catch his breath.

"Where have you girls been the entire damn day?" he shouted.

Laura shrugged but gave no response, while Susie took a break from tending to her toys to answer her father. "We've been playing in here since we left the front yard."

"You almost gave me a heart attack just looking around for you two," he barked before sipping from his beer bottle. Max plopped into the bedroom chair and closed his eyes for a moment.

Susie motioned to Laura silently, and both got to their feet without a single word. They knew it was time to leave.

Laura was relieved; she had managed to stay away from his dirty grip since he arrived. It had been her idea to get into the house through the backdoor and not through the front, so they could tiptoe to Susie's bedroom without him noticing. It took Max a while to figure that one out.

"Good! You two are here!" Aunt Penny, beaming, said as the girls joined her in the kitchen. They had arrived just in the nick of time to help her with dinner.

Aunt Penny looked at Laura and said, "You've been such a big help this week. Why don't you go watch some TV? I think *Who's the Boss* is on."

Laura's skin crawled at the thought of being asked to sit in the same room as her Uncle Max. Surely, he'd be plopped back on the couch soon enough. Her insides churned, and her throat stiffened at the idea that he would, without a doubt, touch his disgusting hands on her delicate skin as he had done before.

"Please!" Laura begged without realizing it, "I can do anything in the kitchen!"

She wasn't lying; Samantha had taught Laura the basics about running a kitchen and even some cooking tips. It was a virtue Samantha had constantly hammered home to Laura.

Aunt Penny smiled, waved Laura over, and said, "Ok, you can peel the potatoes, but you should get busy. I don't want dinner to be late!"

Peeling potatoes isn't an easy task, but Laura would choose to peel a million potatoes rather than sit for one second with that despicable man.

An hour passed, and Aunt Penny was setting out the dishes when Uncle Max made the oddest demand.

Puzzled, Penny asked, "Are you sure about that?"

He grumbled, nodded his head, and said, "Sure! Let's eat together. It'll be nice."

Susie seemed lost by her father's request, and Laura had never heard him want to eat with the family at the table before.

Penny, motioning for the girls to find a seat at the table, said, "Alrighty then." She thought maybe he was making an effort in their marriage, eating together as a family would be a good first step.

Laura sat closest to Aunt Penny, practically in her lap, while they all ate in silence. Uncle Max shot her endless glances and grumbled incoherently as he ate his meal. Laura could tell she wasn't sitting where he wanted her to.

Not today, you fucking bastard, Laura thought.

"Can Laura and I go to bed early once we're done here?" Susie looked at her mother and asked.

Aunt Penny nodded her head gently. "I don't see any reason why you shouldn't. You girls can watch some TV in there if you'd like but lights out by 10:00 p.m."

Laura and Susie exchanged a subtle smile. For Laura, the day felt perfect. It *was* perfect considering the circumstances.

***

"Are you going to have a shower before going to bed?" Susie asked while drying herself.

Laura shook her head forcefully and pulled on the comforter before crawling into bed. Laura had also chosen to sleep with her clothes rather than change, which felt perfect considering she was a few hours away from leaving the hellish house.

Susie jumped into bed and immediately covered herself with the comforter.

Uncle Max slipped his head through the partly opened door and grinned just before Aunt Penny called out loud to him, "Max! Let the girls be, will you?"

"I'm just saying goodnight!" he yelled before he went out with the guys to the local bar for the night.

TWELVE

The clock in the bedroom had just struck, indicating another hour had passed in the middle of the night. For the last few hours, Laura had counted the seconds, feeling miserable and sickened while she watched the time tick away. She hoped that morning would soon come. Finally, she had managed to watch the clock tick one a.m. before losing her battle with sleep.

Unfortunately, sleep had not been kind to her since Uncle Max returned. Sleep took her away, unable to watch guard. She wished Uncle Max would sleep forever. If only that were possible.

It wasn't the eerie silence that awakened Laura or the fact she could no longer feel Susie's body by her side. It was the sick feeling that came with the ominous odor, so strong it stung her nostrils and dragged her into consciousness, forcing her eyes to open.

"Oh God!" were the words that first escaped the little girl's mouth.

The previous situations paled compared to what she felt she was about to endure. Every action she took before she slept had seemed enough to ensure her safety for one more night. But fate dealt her one final colossal blow.

"Susie!" Laura whispered but hoped she had screamed as she felt for her cousin by the bedside. Next to her were rumpled covers and an empty bed. Susie was gone.

Not now, God, not now. Laura thought. *It's the middle of the night.*

Uncle Max chuckled derisively, leaned himself towards her ear, with his entire weight pressing down hard as he whispered, "Susie fell sick a little bit ago and is with her mother."

Uncle Max was out all night at the bar. He must have just returned and was in rare form, worse than usual. The realization brought Laura's world crumbling down and suddenly dashed into a zillion pieces as she grabbed her pillow and quickly began to understand her present reality.

"It's just you and me now," he said perversely.

Laura wanted to fight and shove him off her body, but it felt like the wind had been knocked right out of her sails. He was sitting on her back. She wanted to scream and let her voice be heard around the house, but his previous threats about harming her felt like invisible gags placed perfectly across her mouth.

She had been tense and on defense all day long. However, she knew that wicked Uncle Max had won the war even before engaging in the battle.

He had won psychologically and weighed her down emotionally like an anchor hanging from her heart. She had let her guard down during his absence and wasn't prepared for his return.

"You shouldn't struggle," he warned her in a calm, confident voice.

Laura felt like a cornered deer without options while she laid chest down, and her eyes stared blankly at the wall in front of her. She prayed for her soul and her rescue, but Uncle Max chipped away the little strength she had left. Her resolve, like a sandcastle battered by the harsh and endless sea waves, had been beaten beyond recognition.

Laura moved in restriction, not her muscles, but her eyelids as they clamped shut. Hoping and trying not to feel anything in the present, she held still for a moment while she tried to picture memories of herself in the happiest places possible.

Don't let Satan blow it out, I'm gonna let it shine, she sang weakly in her mind. *Don't let Satan blow it out…*

Time felt like it stopped, and the elements slowly began to feel like they were working against her. Finally, Laura parted her eyelids and allowed the burning tears to flow down her cheeks.

Laura whispered, "Please!"

In the single word, the little girl had included everything she held dear, and all she could summon from her existence in hopes it would reach whatever sane side he still had left in him.

Max only replied, "It will all be over soon."

The sound of his zipper coming undone screeched painfully through her ears. She wouldn't fight, or at least, she couldn't even if she wanted to. He had overpowered her strength by kneeling on her back, but he had saddled her resolve and was now holding it in his hands.

Laura wept profusely into her pillow, wondering how many other young girls were dealt the same fate. It felt surreal, and she lacked comprehension. He wasn't about to explain his horrible deeds. Uncle Max would rather show her in the most damning way possible. He would scar her for the rest of her life. His pleasure, her pain. Laura had lost her fight.

Sliding downwards gently so he could be on her thighs, he placed his hand on the back of her head pushing her face into the pillow, and warned, "If you scream, I'll hurt you."

Laura remained there, wondering if he knew she had no screams left. His cold, rough and hardened hands groped her pants and aggressively yanked them down to her ankles, stripping her of the last sense of dignity she had left.

Still not done, he took a moment to savor the sight of Laura in her underwear before slowly slipping them down, too, granting him unrestricted access to her buttocks.

Laura squirmed but couldn't fight. Instead, she closed her eyes once again and made wishes she knew only genies in magic lamps could grant. She would wish upon him the most painful and damning death possible.

"Now, that's lovely." His perverted words ran out in a slithery whisper as he squeezed her buttocks inside his hands. "Lay still for me. Just lay still for me."

She could feel the sting from his cold hands through her heart like an icicle. He ran his finger along the lining and heaved out sighs of relief and savor. Naked from the waist down, and completely stripped of her dignity, Laura wondered what caused her cousin to fall sick and let the animal now sitting on her enter the room.

Please God! she prayed even though it felt like she wanted to curse aloud. *Please let it end! I will be a good girl. I will let my light shine. I won't let Satan blow it out. Please, let it end.*

All Laura wanted was her family and the comfort of her home. She wasn't going to beg any longer. She wasn't going to give Uncle Max the satisfaction he obviously enjoyed.

Without resistance, he pulled something out of his pants and rubbed it between her thighs. She could feel the fleshy organ slowly gain strength as the seconds passed. He ran his hand underneath her top and along her back. But, for Laura, she couldn't feel anything anymore. Her skin felt dead and defiled, and the only parts of her body that functioned were her heart and eyes.

Through her eyes, she wept sadly, and through her heart, she bled hurt. She clenched her teeth into the pillow while Uncle Max satisfied himself by forcefully parting her legs so that he could gain easier access to her. Laura felt him fiddle her with his fingers and breathe heavily while he held himself in his left hand. Laura wanted to puke her guts out immediately.

"Yes!" he mumbled.

Feeling more tears roll down her cheeks and with her teeth still grinding hard into the pillow, Laura prayed silently to God; *Please take my life! Just take my life now and let this end!*

124

Having God grant her prayer felt like it would be the most merciful gift she could ever receive. She wanted nothing more from life. She simply wanted her life to come to an end. But it didn't. Uncle Max continued for the next few minutes until he suddenly paused.

She could feel him breathe heavily with each passing second and curse in words that only meant he was enjoying his actions.

Laura felt stiffened in every part of her body, and her nerves seemed like they were no longer functioning. She knew it would end and hoped it would be soon, but he still wasn't done, or at least not until he got what he was craving.

Biting her lower lip as she fell short of words to speak, Laura prayed, *Dear God, please help me!*

She wished she could stop breathing. But, instead, each breath burned her lungs and set her throat on fire as she tried to hold still and simply suffocate herself to death in the pillow.

"There... there... just a short while more," he boasted proudly.

He began to jerk and finally, the beast finished. Uncle Max slowly crawled off her body and headed for the door as he always did after getting whatever he wanted. He walked out of the room and left his damning essence littered all over, the most damaging, on Laura.

With her tears all but dried up, and her skin crawling with nothing but disgust, Laura laid still and continued to stare at the wall opposite her. She wanted to leave the house. She left her pants and underwear around her ankles where he had left them, reached for the covers, and pulled them over her body.

Please, God, take my life, she begged in a whisper without opening her eyes.

Laura felt incomplete and defaced. Her entire existence felt like it had been defiled. Her spine trickled with nothing but misery as she prayed not for grace to see her through the night but for merciful death to take away her breath. Satan blew out her light, and she felt it completely extinguish within her.

Alone, hurt, afraid, and feeling terrified beyond what words could possibly tell, she watched the morning sun slowly begin to rear its head. Broken and feeling like the world didn't deserve someone as filthy as her, Laura thought of what it must feel like to be someone else.

I want to die, she thought as her remaining breath failed her, and her consciousness drifted away into an abyss of misery.

Just before her consciousness left her, Laura thought of all the odds stacked against her. Susie fell ill, but Laura had managed to avoid Uncle Max the entire day.

The odds that her parents would bring her back to the damned house.

Laura felt the world wasn't meant for her. She had found a demon in the unlikeliest of places, and he had done his bidding without restriction. As a result, her thick walls were up, and her emotions were utterly stripped away. Any sense of pride or self-love was gone. It was replaced with self-loathing and anguish. Laura wasn't sure if she could trust anyone or herself ever again. The world didn't feel right, and it might never feel right again.

Thirteen

T he Psalm "weeping may endure for a night, but joy cometh in the morning," sounded farfetched and impossible for Laura. Her eyes glued their focus on the wall as she heard the door slowly creak open behind her. Normally, she would have turned to see who had just come in, but it didn't matter anymore. She felt there was no longer anything precious about her. The thought had drifted into her consciousness all night and eventually mixed with every ounce of blood coursing through her veins. The house no longer scared Laura; instead, it filled her with her accepted misery.

She heard Susie cough and slide into bed with her. "You look pale," Susie whispered before letting out another cough.

Susie truly was sick, her illness wasn't her fault, but Laura still wanted to blame her for every misdeed when she came to visit her house. She had felt her precious dignity become stripped and fed to a dog of no virtue. It wasn't anyone's fault, but Laura wanted someone or something to blame. Anger began to curb the pitiful pleas for death, and a determination arose inside her.

Gently getting into an upright position, Laura's expression was bland for a moment, she looked at her fingers and held back the teardrops threatening to come crawling down her face. Laura had wept quietly all night long, and her entire body felt dehydrated. She felt she might have passed every drop of water she possessed through her eyes.

"I have to go," Laura whispered, getting to her feet, and tossing the comforter aside.

Still having her pants and underwear around her ankles, where Uncle Max had left them, she walked over to her suitcase and began searching for her clothes. Yanking out some new sweats and a top, she began to change. She could smell Uncle Max's distasteful aura and sweat as she packed the items back into her bag.

Confused, Susie got to her feet and reached out to touch Laura, but she had no idea how angry her cousin felt. It had taken one more night of emotional torture to break Laura completely. Susie's hand barely rested on Laura's shoulder when Laura snapped and slapped her hand away. Grinding her teeth, Laura turned back with blood-red eyes and clenched fists.

"Do not touch me," were the only words Laura could muster.

Susie held her hands high and slowly began to retreat. She could see that Laura didn't want to be messed with. Emptiness appeared to be swirling in Laura's eyes. Laura dragged her feet toward the door and stopped but never looked back at the room or Susie. She had so many words to say but didn't know how to say them.

I'm sorry, for snapping at you, she thought to say to Susie, but the words just didn't come out.

Feeling dejected like life's new Frankenstein, she continued walking along the hallway leading to the living room. Laura barely looked toward her Aunt Penny's bedroom as she passed and couldn't have cared less if the lady had seen her.

I need to leave, Laura said in her head.

Her bag dragged across the ground. It felt heavier by the second as her weary frame moved toward the door.

"Laura," Aunt Penny said from her rocking chair. Startling Laura, who had not seen her.

She wanted nothing more to do with the family and needed a way out as soon as possible. She wanted to go home. She no longer wanted to be inside the yellow rancher house.

"I'm ready to go home now. Do you know when my parents are coming?" Laura asked her Aunt Penny blank-faced without her usual respectful tone.

Aunt Penny was puzzled but didn't move from her seat. Instead, she rocked herself to a halt and waved at Laura to come over.

"Can I call my mom?" Laura said, her voice louder than the previous time as she tightened her grip around her bag.

Aunt Penny replied, "You don't look so good. Did you get sick in the middle of the night, like Susie?"

Laura felt sick without a doubt, but not the kind of sick that some common cold and cough medicine would cure. She ailed of the stale air within the treacherous house of horrors. She ailed of the shame and the ache within her body. She ailed of feeling like she was nothing but a used, dirty soul wandering the earth, bound to be unloved.

"Laura!" Aunt Penny said again.

Aunt Penny reached her hand towards Laura, barely touching her as the girl shuddered.

"Your mom and dad should be here soon," she said gently. "Why don't you get some water and lie on the couch. Maybe you've got the same bug as Susie."

Laura simply managed a weak smile at Aunt Penny whose husband was the cause of her misery. Laura wished things were different because she enjoyed visiting Susie. She wished Susie's house was a haven and not the devil's lair. Laura lay down on the couch in a fetal position satisfied with the knowledge that her mother and father would arrive soon.

***

Sitting on the front porch for the last thirty minutes did nothing but leave Laura with the same question over and over. *Should I tell them? How would I even begin to tell them?*

She did not want to return to the house ever again. She was not sure if she could share the reason. Her mind was racing with the consequences of anything she might say to her parents.

Damn the consequences! Laura thought.

She brushed her hair out of her eyes. When the familiar car drew down the street, Laura felt a breeze of joy. She had missed her mom and dad immensely, and she looked forward to seeing them. But, just as the car stopped a few feet from her, her eyes welled with tears, and her lips began to tremble.

"Baby!" Samantha said to her daughter in a warmhearted tone. "We've missed...." Samantha saw Laura's tears and said, "Awww, it's ok, we're home now."

As her mother's arms reached for her, Laura flinched and pulled her head backward, but not enough to prevent the woman from making contact. The warm feeling from Samantha's hug felt different and seemed to be exactly what Laura needed. She wrapped her arms around her mother's waist immediately and planted her head into her chest while she sobbed endlessly.

Samantha brushed her hand down her daughter's hair and whispered, "I know you missed us, and we missed you too. We can go home now."

"We should say goodbye to your Aunt Penny and Uncle Max." Samantha motioned towards the door but stopped upon realizing her daughter was fighting against moving with her.

"NO! NO! NO!" Laura cried aloud. "I just want to go home! I just want to go home now! Please let's go home!"

Baffled, Samantha paused and watched the storm door open while Aunt Penny and Susie stepped out. Uncle Max followed behind with Laura's belongings and loaded them in the powder blue Mercedes.

"I think someone is ready to go home," Samantha said as she chuckled. "It seems the girls had loads of fun, but perhaps the time away from home has been a little too long. Laura is ready to go."

Laura felt relieved to get in the car. Finally, *I'm free*, she thought. She felt her tears begin to slowly fade.

Samantha looked at Laura and asked, "What is wrong with you, honey?"

Laura wiped the last of her tears and stared blankly at her mother. She wondered what the woman would think, say, or even do if she told her about the events that had occurred in the house. Laura wanted to tell her so badly, and everything within her screamed for her to let it out.

Chills of fear and terror filled her guts, and she choked on the words she had hoped to spill to her mother. Currently, Uncle Max caused Laura pain, and only Laura. But she knew that if she told Samantha, it would cause a lot of pain for everyone else.

"Are you going to talk to me?" Samantha said once again.

Laura wondered if she could simply answer and let everything come crashing down. Painfully, her mind had frozen in an endless replay of every single incident from the first day he made his sickening move. Laura had hoped she could gain the courage to tell her mother.

"I'm so happy to be heading home. I really missed you guys," she managed to squeak out.

For the entire ride home her broken mind, like a tape on an endless loop, recounted every dreadful event time and time again. She couldn't move, and she couldn't blink, but she could see Uncle Max inside her head, hear his zipper, and perceive the stench from his alcohol-drenched breath and body. Laura had left Uncle Max's house, but he was still present in her head.

***

Anticipating Laura's return, Paul danced around the living room. He missed his little girl and couldn't wait to see her. This trip had been the first time Paul and Samantha left Laura for that many days. They did travel a lot, but typically small, few day trips. Paul carried all the luggage into the house while Samantha went to pick up Laura. The sun was bouncing off his dark receding hair through the skylight in the ceiling. The large living room seemed so empty without anyone home. Just then, he heard the courtyard gate creek and ran to the door to greet his girls.

Paul opened the door with his arms wide, Laura slowly walked inside. He reached for her, and she could feel her body tense. His touch was uncomfortable at first, but he was her father. It only took a moment for her to relax and fall into his arms. Laura, letting out days of locked-up emotions, had tears begin to stream down her face again. Her emotions had been bottled up so tight it was like a cork had popped from a champagne bottle. Laura felt so good to be home.

Paul said, "Let me look at you, are you ok? What's the matter?"

Before Laura could answer, Samantha said, "She did the same to me when I picked her up. I think she really missed us."

Paul scooped Laura up into his arms and started twirling her around the room, he said, "We love you and missed you, love you and missed you, bunches and bunches and bunches."

Paul twirled her into the living room and sat on the couch with Laura beside him. On the coffee table sat a beautiful statue of the Blessed Mother.

"This is Our Lady of Medjugorje," Samantha said proudly.

The figure was about 12 inches tall. Wearing a flowy blue dress and a white veil, Our Lady stood atop blue and white clouds with her right hand over her heart and her left hand outstretched. Her head was tilted downward and adorned with a beautiful halo.

"We brought this for you to put in your room. She will watch over you at night," Samantha said.

If only I had her a few days ago, Laura thought. She hated herself for thinking it. The statue was beautiful.

Samantha looked at her husband, and they both wore the same baffled expression on their faces. Samantha said, "Laura honey, I know you missed us, and we missed you too, but are you sure that everything is ok?"

Laura thought about the question again and felt the words dance on her lips but was unable to speak. She thought again about how much pain she was in and how that pain would multiply if others knew what had happened. Laura also knew that she could not return to Susie's ever again. She had to tell them something. She had to figure out a way to let them know she never wanted to go back to Susie's again.

"You can talk to us, honey," her father said in an encouraging tone.

Staring at Our Lady on the table, Laura's heart skipped a beat as she responded, "Uncle Max kissed me."

It wasn't anywhere near what she wanted to say, but it was the best she could summon. She looked up into her mother's eyes, but the woman didn't seem perturbed.

"Is that what's making you sad?" Samantha asked.

Laura nodded and lied again. "He kissed me on the lips, and it made me feel very uncomfortable," she said.

The lie had stuck, and it was the best she could muster.

Her father rubbed her back, drew her closer, and said, "You must have mistaken the intent behind his kiss, darling."

Laura's hairs stood up on her neck, and her shoulders raised a few inches. Paul's touch on her back made her jolt back to Uncle Max's vile deeds, but she continued staring at Our Lady.

"Could he have pecked you on the cheek and accidentally hit your lips? Is that possible?" Paul asked.

Devastated beyond words, the ordeal sank her heart. She wondered what their response would be if they had heard the truth. She also wondered if she'd go to hell now, since she just flat out lied in front of Our Lady. The Catholic guilt filled her up inside. Part of her wanted to tell them the truth, but she decided to keep it a secret. However, she needed a reason never to go back. She had to do something.

"I didn't have a good time, it was too long, and I don't want to go back!" Laura said in protest and got to her feet as she raced for her room. "I never want to go back there ever again!"

Samantha shouted after her daughter, "Okay, okay, you don't have to go there again, sweetie!"

FOURTEEN

Fall 1989

Two years had passed, and the memories of the stench and horror at Susie's house had slowly faded into the dark recesses of Laura's mind, but they still lurked, ready to return at any moment. Laura would never be safe from the reach of her memories. She had suffered through years of teachers' reprimands and poor grades that disappointed her parents. What had happened to their perfect child?

Laura remained rooted in the middle of the Catholic School hallway, watching the other kids scurry to the tune of the school bell as they hurried towards their classrooms to avoid getting into trouble. It was her first day of eighth grade. Hoping she would adjust better each time, Laura's parents had switched her school each year for the past two years.

Besides the warm smile Samantha had given, there had been words of wisdom to follow, and many of them hinged on her being a "better" little girl. "Life is going to give you lemons," Samantha always said, "but you have to take those lemons and turn them into lemonade, Laura. You must always keep your glass half full, Laura. Life is what you make it, Laura." Like most girls entering their teen years, they didn't want to listen to anything their mothers said. Laura wasn't any different.

Unfortunately, Laura had lived the past few years being a shadow of her old self. Sighing and somewhat disinterested she mumbled, "Let's get this over with."

Dressed as sharply as she could in her brand-new school uniform, she tried to prepare herself for what another year at school would feel like. Laura couldn't help but feel the overwhelming effects of everything.

Seeing the other kids laugh and begin to pair themselves into cliques of friends unsettled her. She was already running on damaged confidence and an introvert's personality. She stood and stared at the walls in the hall, freshly painted and ready for the new school year. Everything was like a shiny new penny. The teachers had placed brightly colored decorations to create feelings of welcome in their classrooms. The school motto was hanging for everyone to see: "Be Kind. Be Respectful. Open Your Mind to Learning."

What if they see me as nothing but tragic? she thought to herself. *What if they find out my secret?*

There were rules to conform with, and she was breaking one by standing in the hallway and not entering her classroom. Laura dragged her feet and walked towards the end of the hall where Mr. Benton taught her class.

She had spent the previous night battling with the feeling of being nothing but a non-entity and an odd duckling. She was not in sync with anything around her. She preferred the comfort of her home and the embrace of her family. From the moment she stepped out from her mother's car, an overwhelming feeling had set in, and it didn't seem like she would be able to shake it.

"Hey! Young lady!" a rather bold and commanding tone said aloud from behind, prompting Laura to halt but not look back. "HELLOOO!"

Laura heard the teacher shouting, but she continued to walk toward her class and ignored whoever was calling.

The footsteps behind her quickened and brought her face-to-face with a frowning teacher with burly features as he leaned closer and said, "I was talking to you, missy. What's your name?"

Laura looked up at him slowly, ground her teeth against one another, and breathed out a sigh without answering the man.

"Are you new here?" he asked in a frustrated tone. "You shouldn't be out here in the hallway."

He reached over to lead her by her hand, but Laura yanked herself free and began brushing against the spot where he had touched her.

"Don't ever touch me again," Laura yelled and frowned at the befuddled-looking teacher who stood with his hands on his hips, and his eyes widened as he stared down at her.

Laura stormed off, leaving the displeased teacher behind. He watched her as she stopped before classroom 202. Being snarky and rude with the teachers came so naturally to Laura now.

As she entered the room, the spot on her arm was still tingling from the teacher's touch. Uncle Max was in her past, but she still felt him in every touch.

"Hello," said Mr. Benton standing in front of the class with a marker in his hand as he smiled and waved at her. "You need to be in my class on time. Go find your seat now."

Laura nodded and looked back at the row of seats. The classroom was filled with brown desks, each partnered with a green metal chair. The desks were occupied in such a way that whichever seat she chose, she would feel boxed in. She felt like a sore thumb.

Most students had formed their friendship groups previously and were already sitting together.

"You can take the first seat on the front row," Mr. Benton instructed but watched Laura ignore him as she made her way to the back of the class. She slammed her bag onto the table and caused a stir in the quiet room.

Casting her different facial expressions and thought-filled looks, everyone turned and looked at Laura as she slipped herself into the vacant seat. The group of girls just behind her giggled and laughed horridly as she sat down.

"Hey, you," one of them wearing a pink ribbon in her hair and what appeared to look like mild lip gloss smeared across her lips called out.

"What's your name?" the girl asked.

Laura didn't initially seem sure she wanted to answer. Instead, she looked away and picked at her cuticles nervously. Laura formed the bad habit a while ago. She wasn't sure when it started, but she picked her cuticles often, sometimes until they bled.

"My name is Laura." She replied in a whisper so faint it was almost impossible to hear.

"Looks like the new girl can't speak her name," said a tall, olive-skinned girl sitting a few seats from Laura. The others laughed and teased her before the teacher called their attention back to the front of the class.

Feeling her face flush red with anger, and her eyes swell with tears, she yanked her bag from the chair and raced out of the class without asking permission. The girls' laughter echoed from where they sat.

"Come back here!" Laura heard Mr. Benton shout to her, but Laura ran as fast as her legs could carry her down the hall.

Feeling unable to hold back the tears, Laura barged into the girl's restroom, tossed her bag onto the floor, crawled into a stall, and slammed the door shut behind her as she fell to her knees and wept bitterly. Her heart was racing faster than it normally should, and she had begun hyperventilating at the thought of having to be in that classroom again.

The students seemed different from her, not necessarily different, but she felt they had an air of superiority over her, and she wasn't sure how to manage their judgments of her.

They don't know me, so why do they judge me? I just need to survive this year. If I can fit in with the cool crowd, then maybe, just maybe it'll be okay, Laura thought.

She wept on the bathroom floor and prayed. *Why me, God!? Why me?*

The question lined her lips and riddled her thoughts as the class bell rang. She heard the bathroom door open, and footsteps made their way inside.

"Who saw Jack walk into class earlier today looking like a hottie?" one girl said before clapping her hands and encouraging some shrieks from the other girls.

Laura froze as she realized one of them was the same girl that had goaded her in class earlier. She wasn't entirely sure, but she remained in the stall. She kept quiet. Barely even making a sound with her breath, she hoped they would do their business and leave.

"Hey guys, look," one of the girls said. "Isn't this that new girl's backpack?"

Laura searched around the green-tiled stall for her backpack and realized she had tossed it angrily to the ground outside the stall. Unsure what to do, she remained hidden and decided she'd continue to wait it out rather than reveal herself.

"Laura!" one of them shouted, "At least, that's what it says here on your school identification card."

Ramming the back of her head into the stall's wall, Laura held her breath while the girls poured out her backpack rudely.

"Are you going to come on out, or should we just trash the items in your backpack?" Another asked.

Laura felt her heart skip. She thought of rushing out to claim her belongings but decided to stay put. The girls knocked on the stalls and opened them to determine where she was hiding. Laura knew they would soon catch up to her. She stepped out, managed the bravest possible face she could summon, and shouted with attitude, "That's mine. Give it to me!"

Laura, angry and daring, looked straight into the girls' eyes. The girls slowly circled her like vultures. They stared down at her with their height granting them the advantage.

The tallest of the trio smiled and stared at the olive-skinned girl with pretty, long hair.

"Sheila, what do you say we make the new girl our friend?" she asked.

Laura, holding her ground, saw Sheila cringe at the thought and spit distastefully to the ground immediately. It was despicable, to say the least. Laura had tolerated so much in her life at this point, she had gotten comfortable with despicable, and it just didn't matter.

Angry but drained of confidence, Laura could have sworn her lips were about to spill words in plea to be accepted into their group and become their friend. They were popular or at least gave off the aura of popularity. Laura wanted to be accepted. She thought it might help her see past the damages scarring her soul.

Sheila stepped closer and ran her finger along Laura's face. Laura cringed and flinched at the touch.

Sheila said, "I assume we can take her in, but she has to show she wants it more than anything else. She must be willing to do whatever we ask."

Laura remained silent while the blonde girl sneaked her hand into her own bag and took out a lipstick that she handed over to Sheila

"Sheila!" the first girl called. "It might get her in trouble."

Sheila didn't seem to care as she held out the lipstick and giggled excitedly. Laura looked Sheila square in the eyes and stretched out her hand.

"Show us you really want to be friends, and we'll think about it," Sheila said to Laura.

Laura thought briefly about the consequences of her future actions. She figured it might be her one chance at making friends. She walked over to the mirror on the wall and looked back at Sheila, who waved her on and smiled.

The blonde-haired girl stood by Sheila laughing. The third girl threatened to step forward and stop Laura.

Sheila stepped in and said, "Come on, Sonia, it's all in good fun. Don't ruin it. Let's see what guts the new girl has."

Laura choked down hard. Her confidence was beginning to fade, but her determination didn't waver. Her hand trembled as she put the edge of the opened lipstick to the mirror. It felt wrong, Laura knew it, but she continued anyway. Her day so far in school had not been the merry and cherry topping her mother had promised her for the past few weeks. Laura thought about her mother's words.

Things will get better at this school, she said.

You will make new friends, she said.

You will get excited about meeting boys, she said.

You will enjoy learning like you used to, she said.

Laura felt the farce in all those words now. She hurried to write the words onto the mirror. She hoped her new classmates would approve of the proposed friendship.

Sheila stepped closer and said, "You have to make it personal... put your name, so we know you mean it."

Laura halted and considered how silly the idea was, but she nodded and scribbled her name beneath the sentence she had written. Making a mockery of Laura, the three girls moved closer, stared at the scribbled words on the mirror, and burst into laughter.

Pointing a finger at Laura, Sheila chuckled and said, "I didn't believe you would do it, but damn!"

Sonia seemed less amused, but it didn't stop her from sharing in the fun as she laughed hard and almost fell to the ground.

Laura had not realized it, but her mind had ordered her hand without granting her brain the opportunity to think things through. She mumbled the words softly, as she read the words out loud.

Mr. Benton is a loser… Laura.

Laura turned to the girls and asked, "So, am I part of the group now?"

Sheila scoffed. She waved at her friends, and they all walked out of the bathroom together. Laura stood in the empty room, she felt alone and betrayed. She was somewhat desperate to have her inner voice heard as she cried aloud but remained silent. Laura would have normally started to sob, but she was mostly full of bitterness and anger.

Laura packed the spilled contents of her backpack and fought back her tears. She heard the bathroom door open again. She didn't bother to look because she assumed it was the three mean girls who had proposed to be her friends. Suddenly, an elderly scent hit her nostrils and she could see the older women's black shoes.

"Are you responsible for this?" the woman asked with her hand pointed in the direction of the lipstick on the mirror. Laura froze and saw it was one of the nuns standing before her. She was frowning and obviously displeased by the message on the mirror.

Trying to summon up a credible lie, Laura stuttered, and said, "It wasn't me. I found it this way. Some girls dumped out my backpack."

It sounded true enough, but there was a chink in the armor of such a crudely cooked-up lie. The nun walked over to the mirror and read it out loud. "Mr. Benton is a loser…Laura"

As she turned to face Laura, she stepped on the identification card.

She leaned over to pick it up, stared at Laura with a raised brow, and said, "Laura Shirk it says on the card. What is your name, child?"

Laura was beginning to hate that question, and she chose to remain silent. The image clearly displayed on her card did well enough to give her away as the Laura who scribbled on the mirror. But she refused to give any vocal clarification as she frowned and held her backpack close to her chest.

"Well, since you don't seem to have any recollection of what your name is, young lady," the woman cleared her throat and said, "you're spending your lunch with me."

***

Laura had no idea what sort of punishment she would get, but she assumed it would not be anything fun. She trailed the nun as she strolled around the lunchroom until she found a suitable seat at the table with the other teachers. Laura's first day at her new school was getting worse as the minutes passed.

The lunchroom was filled with students going about eating their meals. The teachers remained segregated from the students sitting on the opposite side of the room. For Laura, sitting with the teachers brought with it the miserable feeling of being caged in. To make things worse, the mean girls who had claimed to want to be her friend laughed at her from where they sat across the lunchroom.

Rolling her eyes, Laura tried to focus on her meal and hopefully drown everything else out. It was not easy. She felt burdened at heart and in her soul with issues she could not explain. She used to like being at school, and she wished there was a school where she could feel right at home.

The students looked so happy and carefree, and she craved that, or at least, she felt envious of it because she could feel it absent within her. She wondered what sort of homes they all grew up in and whether they encountered dangerous men like her Uncle Max.

"Laura!" the nun called out for the third time.

Laura had confined her consciousness into a place farther away from the lunchroom. The nun was frustrated at her inability to get through to Laura and gently laid her hand to rest on top of Laura's. The nun watched Laura suddenly grow conscious of her surroundings and yanked her hand free.

"Don't touch me!" Laura said aggressively.

"Are you all right?" the concerned-looking nun asked.

Laura could read the expression of pity slowly crawling across the women's face, and she nodded her head as much as she could to dispel the notion that she wasn't okay.

"This isn't an ideal way to begin your first day, and if you keep up with the shenanigans I saw in the bathroom earlier, things might get difficult for you here," the nun explained. "You can call me Sister Garcia."

Laura nodded her head; however, it wasn't in compliance, but more in a way to get her to stop talking.

"Finish your meal and return to class as soon as you're done," Sister Garcia said. "I will be keeping a close eye on you, young lady."

Laura realized she had gotten herself a disciplinarian who obviously would haggle her around the school if she kept getting out of line. To make things worse, the male teacher, whom she had acted rudely to earlier, continued to shoot rather curious stares her way from the end of the lunch table, and it would only be a matter of time before Mr. Benton found out she called him a loser.

God, help me, Laura thought while she battled with her food for the next half hour.

Nothing felt right. If middle school wasn't bad enough for most, Laura felt shameful and alone. She could not wait for the dismissal bell to ring; she was ready to go home.

***

The air was warm, and the sidewalk stretched along the length of the entire main street just outside of the school. Laura sat outside and waited for her mother's car to pull to a halt. It felt like an eternity, even though only a few minutes had passed since the bell rang. Laura spent the last few hours in class being teased by the mocking gaze of what felt like everyone. She wanted out of the school as soon as possible.

Why am I not like them? she had asked herself.

By her own validation, she was nothing and stood in contrast to the cool kids in her class. They all seemed to have interesting topics to speak about. Yet, she was left peddling remnants of their information. She wondered what it would feel like to have people completely invest themselves in her without trying to take advantage of her. The reality was their judgments weren't entirely their fault.

Laura was weird; she was someone the other kids couldn't understand. If she were honest with herself, she didn't trust any of them anyway.

They are just kids, she had tried to convince herself.

Laura tried to talk to a boy named Ryan but fell short of words when she assumed he had looked down on her too.

To Laura, there was an invisible wrath of doom following her around, and she could not shake off the feeling that she had picked it up from her Uncle Max's smelly house. Her self-worth seemed to have taken a steep nosedive, while her inner voice cried to be heard, but nobody was listening, or at least, that was how it seemed.

When her mother's car pulled to a stop before her, Laura leaped to her feet. She felt loved by her mother and was glad to be headed home. Her heart burst with joy, and her steps had enough springs in them to propel her over the car.

Samantha leaned over, planted a kiss on her daughter's forehead, and asked, "How was school today, darling?"

Laura thought about the appropriate answer to the question.

"School was good," Laura lied and managed a smile she had mastered for times spent around her family.

They still had no idea the mental torment she endured. Some days, she thought she'd explode all her thoughts and feelings in hopes it would help her ease off the burden. But Laura remembered how her folks downplayed "the kiss." It made her cower in fear to tell the entire truth. She thought about the pain that telling her secret would cause her family and that only made the desire to keep quiet grow stronger.

"I don't like this school," Laura said to her mother without looking at her.

"Is there something you aren't telling me, sweetie?" Samantha said as she looked at her daughter briefly before turning her eyes back to the road.

Laura wanted to tell her mother about it all; the way she flinched every time someone touched her. The way the girls had been mean to her, how she might have gotten into the bad graces of two, maybe three teachers.

For certain, at least one majorly while the other would keep a close watch on her. Laura had so much to say but with so little courage to spill any of it.

She adopted the self-preserving mechanism she had managed to perfect; Laura smiled and kept a calm face as she replied, "No, Mom. Everything is perfect."

Laura had lied again, and it certainly wasn't going to be the last time.

FIFTEEN

Spring 1990

L aura could see her hands shaking with the report card in them, with a side note giving the details of her misdemeanors at school spread across the three-page document. Samantha flipped through page by page as she read her daughter's transgressions with a frown and a disappointed look on her face. It had been half an hour since she finished reading, and she hadn't said a word.

Laura watched her mother look up but looked back down again as she struggled to maintain a gaze with her daughter for too long. Hostile and unaccommodating were the feelings Laura got from the room as she stood with her back to the wall like an offender waiting to be punished. Wearing a confused look, Paul soon walked into the room in his flannel work shirt and Levi jeans as his wife held out the papers for him to read.

Her father, a noisy reader, spelled out the words in a mumbled tone. He looked away from the papers to glance at his daughter before continuing.

"Mom..." Laura drew closer to her mother but stopped.

The woman was unhappy because she couldn't even look her youngest child in the face.

"Laura?" her father finally spoke and called out to her.

Laura nodded her head but gave no response in words.

"You can read, can't you?" he said as he handed notes from the school to her so she could have a look for herself.

Laura had a sense of everything that had been written in there and would rather not read it, but she wasn't going to disobey her father. That was a line she wouldn't cross, even if she was disrespectful with her teachers in school. Laura read through the pages, from the listings of her terrible grades to her constant issues and clashes with students, teachers, and principals.

The list was endless, but everything within the pages was true, and there was no denying it.

"You got more Cs on this one report card than you've ever gotten since your first day of school," her father pointed out. "Since when did you start getting Cs?"

Laura took another guilty look at the grades and felt she deserved them. Neglecting assignments and refusing to take some tests because they were impromptu meant she would struggle academically and accept the results given to her. However, they were just mid-term tests, and she could hide under the premise that she would buckle down for the remainder of the year.

About to lose it, Paul said, "I want a reasonable explanation from you, Laura!"

Laura looked to her mother for support, but even Samantha needed answers why their previously sweet daughter had turned into a menace at school. Bad behavior and low grades were something not condoned at the Shirk house.

"Please help us understand, Laura," Samantha pleaded.

Laura twitched and sighed. "I tried my best; I really did, but…."

"This isn't your best darling," her mother said. "You've always been the brightest kid in the family, and now, you cannot even do well in math? What is going on with you?"

Laura sighed while attempting to turn around.

"Don't you dare, Missy!" her father warned in a raging tone. "Don't you dare make those noises or try to walk away when we're talking to you! You are grounded. Clearly, that will give you the time to study that you need."

Laura shriveled up on the inside and retreated from her father as she feared the worst. Motioning to her husband that she would sort things out with her daughter, Samantha stepped in immediately. Leaving Laura startled, Paul stormed out the door and slammed it shut behind him.

Samantha turned to her daughter and led her to the couch in the living room. They sat opposite of each other, and her mother reached for her hand with a twinkle of pain and worry in her eyes as she searched for answers from her daughter. Laura hated how her mother must be feeling about her, but her lack of understanding about what troubled her mind remained a huge barrier that Laura wasn't sure they could just shelve aside.

"I am sorry," Laura simply apologized. "I am sorry, Mom."

Samantha pulled her daughter to her body and gently placed her head against her chest. They sat in silence and enjoyed each other's warmth while their minds raced with thoughts on how to handle the situation.

Laura whispered, "I have a favor to ask, Mom."

Samantha nodded her head and encouraged her to speak.

"I have a party to attend with a couple of friends today," Laura whispered. "Can I go?"

Samantha leaned away from her daughter and wore the biggest and most gentle smile yet. "You want my permission so that you can attend a party?"

Laura nodded her head innocently, "Yes."

Her mother shrugged and asked, "This party, who will be attending?"

"My friends from school," Laura replied.

Samantha let go of her daughter and got to her feet as she headed for the kitchen. Laura chased after her for a response and stopped just as her mother picked up a glass and filled it with water to quench her thirst. Nervous and anxious as her mother dallied with her response, Laura grew frustrated and sighed.

"Are you going to allow me to go or not?" she asked impatiently.

Samantha took her time and smiled before looking at her daughter. "First, you have to do your schoolwork, and then there is the issue of apologizing to your father and assuring him you will bring your grades up."

Laura gave it a brief thought and nodded her head after a while. "Schoolwork, check, and apologize to dad, check that too!"

Laura wrapped her arms around her mother excitedly and sighed aloud.

Samantha held out her hand and gently eased her daughter off her body, "Even after that, we still have to talk about your attitude and behavior at school. I'd like to see at least a shadow of the sweet little girl I raised," she said.

Laura knew that wasn't something that would ever happen, but she wasn't going to spoil her chances of going out by telling her mother. The party, which was something Sheila and her crew had been talking about for about a week, was bound to be fun and perfect for her to catch a break from her drab life. More so, Sheila had promised there would be nice-looking boys there. Laura thought she was perhaps making some progress with the girls. Laura waited for the answer her heart wanted badly and smiled sheepishly at Samantha hoping the woman would cave.

Samantha was no idiot, and she could see through her daughter's rue. "One more thing."

Laura nodded and grinned.

"You're still pretty much grounded, just like your father said, there will be other parties," she smiled and began heading for the stairs.

Laura fumed with her arms crossed over her chest and her brows falling downwards in a frown. Her one chance of finally being accepted into the mix seemed to be slipping away, and she felt her parents wouldn't understand. She waited carefully as her mother became engrossed in cleaning her bathroom. She had been working on it before Laura handed her the devastating reports from school.

Laura hurried to her room. She had plans set and nothing was going to stop her.

***

It was nothing short of disappointing, but there was the added feeling of humiliation in ways she couldn't imagine. The plan had been set, and Laura was standing right there, staring at the empty house. Sheila said the party was at 1015 Lee Street, and Laura had sneaked out to attend. Now, not only was her spirit broken but their prank dealt her confidence a rather plummeting blow.

"Why did I even bother?" an exasperated sounding Laura lowered her head to the ground and turned back around as she began walking away from the house.

The cackles and loud laughter suddenly came from the house opposite the street. The familiar faces were none other than most of her classmates who no doubt had come to have a bite at her confidence by mocking her terribly.

"Who would invite you to the party?" a girl cried atop her lungs while the others laughed aloud.

They were all in Sheila's house; they had come to see a movie, making sure Laura was the joke of the evening. To make things worse, her costume did little to help her situation.

"Sheila lied." Laura bowed her head and began walking back home. "There was no costume party."

Dressed as a princess, something she felt was in absolute contrast to who she was, turned out to be nothing but a hoax. The kids jeered and continued to laugh while Sheila stood with her arms crossed and her face beaming with a most satisfactory smile. Of course, she was mean, but Laura never disputed that.

All Laura wanted was to feel like she was part of the group, but truthfully, she didn't want to be like them. She knew they were shallow, mean, and hateful, reflecting their own lack of confidence as they teased practically everyone in the school who wasn't part of their sacred group. Even though life had managed to strip her innocence and defile her spirit, she wanted to be just another ordinary kid.

Sixteen

Oddly, she found peace in detention; the one place meant to be a reform room for her and to give her ample time to rethink her choices. Slowly and steadily over the year, it had become her sanctuary, somewhere she felt at home. Mrs. Kelley's room served as the after-school detention room; she was the Health & PE teacher. The walls were covered with posters about good nutrition and exercise. Mrs. Kelley checked in the students and sat at her desk. "I have a meeting in a few minutes. DO NOT leave this room or you will be suspended. I will be back to check on you soon," she announced to the group. Leaving the students to fend for themselves, Mrs. Kelley picked up her briefcase and exited the room.

Laura sat upright in her seat and stared at the door blankly while the other kids in the room bickered and laughed over their sexual escapades and other illicit activities. She listened to every word with a desperately beating heart and a rather piqued interest as to what it must feel like to have someone like you or flirt with you.

Through her thoughts and her dulled mind, as she drowned herself in loneliness, Laura heard Jason, her classmate, ask, "Laura, have you had sex?"

Her neck was stiff, and she was too terrified to turn around. Laura cringed and continued picking at her cuticles. She dug her fingers into her lap which slightly raised her plaid uniform skirt. Her stomach felt a sudden rush of discomfort, and her lips remained sealed to hide her tongue, which was glued to the underside of her mouth. She was trapped in between telling the truth and risking the chance of being labeled a loser or simply going with the flow and lying about having sex and being seen as someone funky and fun in his eyes. The question seemed too hard for her to answer.

The other guys with Jason began walking over to Laura. Beginning to sweat now and feeling her fingernails dig into her thighs, Laura whispered in her head, p*lease don't come near me… please… please… please!* Standing in front of her, Jason smiled as he bent over to look into her eyes. She was nervous and the sweat now started to glisten all over her face.

"So, which is it?" he asked. "Have you had sex, or are you still pretty much a virgin?"

For most kids their age, the question would have been inappropriate and entirely wrong. But since Uncle Max became her devil, nothing phased her. It wasn't a perfect world, and Laura knew that all too well. After-school detention was the place set aside for the rascals in the entire school and for those who didn't want to fit in regardless of how hard the school had tried.

Jason, for one, was living up to his reputation for being a pervert. He had been accused of inappropriate sexual advances and innuendos towards girls almost all the time. While he denied the accusations, he found himself in detention weekly because he couldn't help himself. To his right was James, a sweet-faced kid, often too shy to speak, but with a terrible record for skipping class and roaming around the streets with boys from his neighborhood.

Then, there was Larry, the only child of a divorced mother struggling to make ends meet. Her lifestyle of creeping around with different rotten men wasn't setting a positive example for how a man should treat a woman or doing her son any psychological good. He never really spoke, but when he did, his words were filled with filth and inappropriate claims of what he had witnessed his mother doing.

Because they were in a Catholic School, trying to help such students attain a better life by believing God would save them was always the goal. Laura could not count the number of times she had been sent to the school chapel to say confession and pray as well as clean the pews.

171

"Laura! Laura!" Jason called out to her in desperation to get a much-awaited answer. "Have you had sex before or not?"

Laura watched him slowly try to reach for her face, but she brushed his hand off aggressively and with a direct tone she said, "Don't touch me, asshole!"

Suddenly, the door creaked aloud, and they all turned to see three familiar figures enter the classroom.

"Yes," Laura answered as she rolled her eyes and felt her breath almost escape her entirely.

The mean trio who had tormented her life for the past year was in the room now, and because they had arrived, things were about to get a lot worse.

"She said yes," Larry said to Jason, who turned around and stared at her in disbelief.

"No shit!" Larry said as he smiled and giggled excitedly.

Sheila interjected immediately and asked, "Who said yes and to what?"

It was evident that Laura was the only girl in the room before they arrived, but as always, Sheila did her best to demean Laura's existence.

Laura waved her arms aggressively and hoped none of the boys would talk, but Jason spilled immediately, "Laura claims she's had sex before."

Sonia coughed and almost fell to the ground as she burst into rather retch-inducing laughter. Sheila and the other girl soon followed suit, and they infected the boys with their laughter too. Except for James, he didn't seem to think it was funny. Laura looked towards the door and wished she could make a run for it.

She had served a whole week of detention, so ditching on the last day wasn't worth it, especially when the penalty would be an extra week added to her punishment or the suspension Mrs. Kelley had threatened earlier.

"Who'd want anything to do with you?" Sonia asked in a despicable and quite disgusting tone that displayed her feelings across her face.

Laura stepped closer but held her anger. Sonia was a bitch, nothing more, nothing less. She needed to make everyone around her feel less than her, but Laura wouldn't stoop to her level. She had been through much worse. Yes, she wanted to fit in, but Laura would never be a mean girl.

Her heart ached, and her stomach gurgled in despair as she watched them circle her like vultures waiting to use something she might or might not say against her.

"She's just a liar seeking attention," Sheila finally brushed it off. "You wouldn't even know what a penis is."

"Of course, I do!" Laura raged right back at them.

"No you don't!" Sheila yelled back.

Holding off the desire to clock them all in the face, Laura spoke loudly, "I do too! Perhaps not as well as the three of you, since I'm pretty certain you have been with every boy in school. I'm surprised you aren't diseased by now." She said more than she wanted to, but her words were true. Sheila brushed Laura's words off and turned around as the trio went to sit on the opposite side of the room.

"I'm bored," Sonia complained while running her fingers through her hair.

"How about we play a game?" Larry asked.

His words caught their attention, and they all turned around and stared at him, all except for Laura. She was too annoyed to even look his way out of fear the girls might descend on her once again. She just wanted to be normal, to feel normal. She wanted to know that she was worthy of someone's love. Her feelings tore her apart from within. She couldn't understand why the only form of intimacy she seemed fit to receive would be from her deranged Uncle Max. She didn't know how she would ever allow anyone to touch her naked body.

What is wrong with me? she had asked herself countless times, but the question always lingered, unanswered.

"We could play seven minutes in heaven!" Larry finally suggested.

"We should have at least 45 minutes before Mrs. Kelley comes back to check on us," he said as he walked over to his backpack and took out an empty bottle of beer. This brought him absolute praise from the others and recognition that he was a cool kid in their eyes.

"I'm in," Sheila smiled.

Sonia raised her hand too, while everyone agreed but never looked at Laura for her answer.

Trying not to stutter, she held her hand up slightly and whispered, "I will… I'll play too."

The room fell silent, as surprised stares shot her way. She could read the hate in their eyes, except for James, who simply looked shyly away and to the ground.

"No chance in hell," Larry replied.

James stepped in and spoke, "If she isn't playing, then I'm out too."

Jason shrugged and replied, "Well, whatever, dude, but if the bottle lands on her, I'm not spending even a minute in the storage closet with her."

James remained silent and waved Laura over as they all sat on the floor in a tight circle, except for Laura, whom Jason wouldn't sit too close to. She didn't care, though. She was in the game, and there was no stopping her now. She could never understand why they assumed she would want to kiss any of them anyway.

***

The darkness wasn't the only problem: the boy companion who stood in the closet with her was overwhelming. Upon hearing the door slam shut, the hairs on the back of her neck had stiffened, and Laura clamped her eyes closed and whispered words of assurance that everything was going to be all right. Unfortunately, her heightened breathing suggested she didn't believe herself, and she was probably not going to believe it until she got out of there.

Her nerves twitched uncomfortably, and her heart pounded in her ribcage. She wanted out of the closet but not at the risk of being ridiculed. She wanted away from "him" if possible. Leaving would only confirm everyone's judgmental crappy status of her as a weirdo. In addition, the mean girls were right outside the door to bear witness to her fear of playing the stupid game. It was a conundrum Laura had gotten herself into and she wished she had chosen not to play.

Laura had endless streams of thoughts crawling across her mind as she looked at her feet and nervously back up at the boy standing in front of her. It was the first time she had spent time in a dusty old, tightly cramped closet with a boy. Her feet tapped against the floor nervously while he remained silent and stared back at her. He didn't look like he wanted to be there, and quite frankly, neither did she.

Larry cleared his throat impatiently. "You know how to play this game, right?"

Laura nodded shyly and looked through the closet door slit where she could see the others waiting on them to wrap things up. Laura and Larry had seven minutes, and then the crew would resume the game. Glancing at her watch endlessly, Sheila seemed the most impatient. Jason stood looking gloomy and discontent for reasons unknown.

"So, you realize we are supposed to have fun kissing and stuff, right?" Larry asked her to be sure she was aware of how to play the game.

Laura did understand the rules, which is what scared her the most. Watching Larry slowly draw near and close the little space between them, Laura felt the air from her lungs slowly being sucked out of her body, and she stiffened even more. Laura's eyes widened immediately. His hand reached for her, but she managed to nudge it away, then she began to hyperventilate, which caused the boy to stop and stare at her.

"That's exactly why everyone thinks you're a weirdo. You know, Laura, the guys and I talk all the time about how pretty you are, but you are always freaking out. Is something wrong with you?" Larry asked.

His words fell deaf on her ears. Laura nodded her head and replied, "I just don't want to do this."

He stared at her in confusion and frowned as he leaned back against the closet wall. "You don't want to make out with me?"

Laura wanted many things without a doubt but allowing him to touch her within the tight space was not one of them, despite what he might have thought.

"No, I don't want to make out with you. I know, it's such a big surprise," she said sarcastically. "Can we just talk?"

Larry recognized a lost cause when he saw one, and without making any further attempt to persuade her, he answered, "Sure, whatever. What do you want to talk about?"

Laura remained silent, and she weighed out what had just happened in her head. A part of her seemed to collapse immediately in disappointment at the fact he didn't bother trying harder or even show signs he would fight to have her. Feeling rejected even though she had asked for it, Laura cursed her luck and wondered what it might feel like to be a girl like Sheila.

She craved the normalcy and the right to be touched without gagging and feeling tormented inside. But standing there, struggling to breathe, Laura felt like she was losing control. Larry waited impatiently and had begun to mumble in discontent. He seemed to be cursing his luck for getting paired with her instead of Sheila or one of the hotter, easier girls.

Laura felt like she was the ugly duckling nobody cared about. She was the reject nobody seemed interested in giving a second glance. Her spirit was broken beyond what could be repaired. Standing there and staring Larry in the face, she wondered what they could do together in the closet, but with the sickening feeling that she just wasn't good enough for him.

For the umpteenth time, Laura asked herself, *why am I not good enough for him? Why isn't he trying harder to kiss me?*

Watching Larry slowly blur through her vision, she slumped against the closet door, causing it to open, and heard the kids yell in fright as they hurriedly grabbed hold of her and led her to one of the seats.

"Get Sister Garcia!" James yelled.

***

Coughing aloud and sucking in air as she slowly opened her eyes, Laura stared at the white light tucked into the ceiling and wondered what had happened to her. She turned her head to the side and surveyed the bed she was sleeping in. She frowned and slowly sat up.

Coughing aloud again, *the school's clinic?* She thought to herself.

The incident leading to her waking up in the clinic remained a blur, but she was sure she had been in the closet with Larry before passing out.

"Oh, you're awake." Sister Garcia said as she walked into the room with the school nurse by her side.

Laura ignored the nun. Sister Garcia had done everything possible to keep her under surveillance and continually reported to her parents about her school activities over the past year.

"Why am I here?" Laura asked the nurse, who seemed more than happy to answer her.

The nurse took a seat by Laura and said, "You seemed to have had some sort of panic attack, and you passed out."

Laura tried to recall the event the nurse spoke about, but she couldn't quite picture it all in her head.

Adjusting in the bed, and slowly placing her feet on the ground, "Can I go now?" Laura asked.

Sister Garcia nodded her head at the nurse and whispered, "Please leave us."

The nurse walked out immediately, and the nun took her seat. Laura stared at the woman and whispered, "Shit," before slipping her foot into one of her shoes.

"You cannot leave just yet," Sister Garcia protested. "You need to tell me what might have caused you to have a panic attack in that classroom."

Laura wished she could, but even if she would, she wasn't telling her truth to a nun. Thinking about the situation now, it wasn't the first time her breath had failed her. There had been one other time, the day she contemplated suicide by possibly drowning herself in the bathtub at her house. It was a thought, and thankfully, it was just a thought before she passed out and found herself slumped by the tub.

"Laura," Sister Garcia gently spoke out to her in a worried but gentle tone. "Is there something you'd like to share with me?"

Laura could see the nun was interested in finding out if foul play was involved in her collapsing. Even if there was any, there was no way on earth she would rat on the others and further jeopardize her shaky relationship with them.

Shaking her head abruptly, she sounded rather rudely, "Your questions aren't necessary. I am fine, and I would really like to leave right now."

Not a stranger to Laura's tantrums, Sister Garcia simply stood up and stepped aside for Laura to walk past her after putting on her shoes.

Choosing not to look back, Laura headed for the door before hearing Sister Garcia clear her throat and call her attention. "By the way, I took the liberty of calling your mother, and she'll be here in a few minutes."

Laura's throat suddenly contracted. Having her mother at school would only mean giving her mom more heartache and disappointment. Her terrible grades, endless detentions, and ongoing disciplinary issues felt like enough torture on such a loving person. Adding the news that her daughter had a panic attack in school would only make her situation worse and bring about more questions.

Laura hated the feeling of her own skin; her life didn't seem like it was hers anymore. Her soul belonged to Uncle Max and the horrible acts she endured from him. She wondered if dying would bring the peace her soul dearly craved. Death seemed to be the only thing that might bring meaning to her life. Perhaps then she could have peace. Middle school had been nothing, but the turmoil of traumatic memories, hormones, and means girls. She needed a way out of middle school desperately. She needed to find some way to move forward. She needed to shed her invisible scars. Laura knew she needed tremendous healing, but she didn't know how to find it.

SEVENTEEN

Senior Year of High School 1994

For Laura, the news had been the storm that came to break an otherwise perfect day. High school was a rebirth of sorts. She felt renewed, even while her demons still lurked underneath and waited for the perfect moment to burst forth. Laura was given a choice between six different Catholic high schools, and her parents took her to visit each one during her eighth-grade year. She felt like she needed a new place where she could start over, so that is exactly what Laura did. She chose a top school in her area that no one else from middle school would attend. It was a melting pot of sorts, with girls from all over the southern part of the state. It was a girl's only school. No boy's allowed.

High school flew by in a blink, and now, she was a week into her senior year. Laura was hanging out with some friends when she got the disturbing upsetting phone call and had let the phone drop from her hand and

185

crash into the ground. Her entire being felt heavy with sadness upon hearing the unfortunate news from her mother.

"I have some terrible news, honey," Samantha said on the phone when she called her daughter.

Laura felt too terrified to ask what the terrible news was, but her mother's sobs fueled her curiosity and interrupted the conversation. Her mother was distraught, and it didn't take long for Laura to fall back into her seat and await the dreadful news. Unfortunately, her heart neglected its primary function of pumping blood for a moment as it too waited for the inevitably horrible news.

Samantha sniffed even longer and gave a long silence that threatened to quake not just her world but that of her daughter's as well.

"Mom! What happened!?" An impatient sounding and shaken Laura demanded to know.

Samantha felt the words were too heavy to speak. She cringed and tightened her hand around the telephone before finally whispering, "Your Aunt Penny has died!"

Like the end of a terrible movie too unbelievable to conceive in thoughts, Laura let the phone fall from her hand as she sucked in some air to get her heart and lungs functioning again. Every inch of her body ached, and it didn't stop as she hurried out from her friend's house. She decided to head back home upon hearing the news.

Aunt Penny cannot be dead, she thought to herself countless times this must be a mistake.

She had heard nothing about the sweet lady being ill. Although Laura had chosen to cut herself off from her Aunt Penny and Uncle Max since her last visit to the yellow ranch years ago, she saw Susie every day at school last year. Susie started attending the same high school during their junior year.

The news didn't sit well with her. Laura was in a state of denial until she arrived home. She denied the truth in the words her mother had shared. All of that changed, the moment she saw Samantha in person.

***

Laura would well recall the day forever, maybe because it was a sad day for the family and a sign that the world wasn't fair. For many like herself, her Aunt Penny's death was nothing short of overwhelming, and she couldn't contain her emotions as she stood at the door and watched her memorial unfold on that cloudy Saturday morning.

Donning an all-around attire of black, with sad eyes and a splotchy face, she felt her nerves stiffen. Laura could not go anywhere near the open casket placed in the center of the church where everyone viewed her Aunt Penny one last time. She could not reconcile the idea of death with someone so peaceful and loving when the world was filled with so much evil.

"Laura," she heard her name called by a shaky and somewhat sad voice.

Laura had not seen her yet and had not envisioned what she would say when she saw the girl who must be feeling the loss the most.

Laura slowly turned around with a somber expression and open arms. "Susie!"

Susie looked pale, devoid of her buoyant expression, and lean to the bone as though she had not eaten for days. Doing well to hide her reddened eyes behind her dark shades, she leaped into Laura's arms and held on tightly with the feeling that she never wanted to let go ever again.

"I'm so sorry," Laura wept in her cousin's arms. "I am so sorry about your mom."

Laura pulled away gently and watched her cousin take off her shades to reveal the devastating pair of eyes behind them. Laura felt so many consoling words on her lips, but none could do justice for how terribly she felt for her Aunt Penny's passing and her cousin Susie's loss.

"We should take our seats now," Samantha urged both girls with her hand on their backs as they walked over to the section designated for family members.

Laura looked over to see her father, who had just walked in with a wailing Max by his side. She looked away hurriedly and noticed Susie walking towards the open casket. Samantha helped Susie away from the casket and to her seat.

"She should be here!" Susie wept bitterly and screamed. "She can't leave me!"

Her death was a tragedy, which had hit hard at a rather unbelievable period in everyone's lives. For Susie, it was a time in her life to start planning her future and making grown-up decisions. Laura had pictured her Aunt Penny at her upcoming graduation from high school. Laura couldn't help but feel sadness for Susie. *Who would protect the girl now? What would her life become without her mother? How could she be expected to live in the house of horrors with Uncle Max all by herself?*

There were so many feelings swirling inside Laura's head. Every picture of Aunt Penny would hang in her frame of mind forever.

"You have to keep it together, Max." Laura heard her father plead with the devil himself as he wept and seemed inconsolable.

Laura turned to look at him with disbelief at how he could show so much emotion when deep down inside, he was nothing but a walking figure of lies, disgust, and wickedness.

Where had he been? How sick was Aunt Penny? Was he taking care of her? Was he the cause of her sickness? The questions continued to swirl around in her head.

You did this! Laura felt her inner voice yell. *You killed her, you son-of-a-bitch!*

She wanted to shout the words out right there in the church, so everyone could see the weeping man for what he was, a hypocrite and a despicable person that never treated Aunt Penny well. But she didn't. She wished the walls could speak for her, and the air coursing through the room could bear testament to the evil in Max and oust him to be a devil in sheep's clothing.

"Come sit, Max," Samantha pleaded with the grieving man.

Laura sulked and felt her inner hurt threaten to implode as he took his seat beside her. She wondered what the world would come to think or say if they knew exactly what he was. She wondered what the people in the church would think if she stood up and shouted the truth from the pulpit in a eulogy.

You bastard! She thought.

The entire room fell silent as the pastor took to the pulpit. Leaving nothing but gifts of discomfort and sadness, the silence grew amidst those present and slowly invaded their hearts as they stared at the good soul gone.

Laura clenched her fists and felt the hairs on her neck stand as her uncle reached for her thigh with his hand, almost as though he was seeking some form of support from her. She nudged his hand away, shot him a scowling look, and did just about enough to assert her dominance and maturity. She let her mind wander briefly of ways that she might try to kill him later because, even now, she could feel the pain he caused coursing through her veins.

She wasn't the timid girl anymore, and she wasn't going to allow anything remotely close to what he had done to her to happen again, but something within her still felt terrified of him. Something within her still trembled upon feeling his touch, or any touch for that matter. As much as she had managed to tuck away the emotions and try not to allow them to rule her life, they were still there, waiting to be unearthed.

God, why? She lowered her head and let some more tears flow.

She wished the heavens would open, grant her wish, take the devil beside her, and let her Aunt Penny live on

191

for better years. Years without him being there to make her life miserable, the sweet woman who never hurt anyone.

Susie suddenly jumped to her feet and raced out of the church, causing everyone to turn and stare at the grieving daughter whose heart could not take being in the same room with her deceased mother.

"Go and check on your cousin, honey," Samantha said. She sent Laura after Susie with the task of being the positive emotional anchor, which was quite ironic since Laura had been pretty much an internal mess most of her life. But she knew how to act, how to hide her feelings, how to keep moving forward. She knew how to turn lemons into lemonade.

Laura gladly leaped to her feet and headed out of the building. She searched the grounds outside for Susie and found her crumbled into a heap at the foot of a large oak tree not far from the church. Hurt and unsure how best to console her cousin, Laura approached her slowly and sat on the ground next to her.

"Remember, when a seagull shit on your mom's arm," Laura whispered, and the girls burst into laughter for only a moment, but the moment was perfect. Those words seemed rather adequate and encompassed everything she could think of in terms of consoling her cousin.

"Why does life have to be so cruel?" Susie looked up at her cousin and sniffed. "Why does it have to punish us and take away the good people who deserve to live?" Laura had a name to add to the list if it was indeed possible for the grim reaper to choose someone else.

Taking in the gentle caress of the late morning breeze, Laura curled up next to her cousin with the realization that their world had lost a good person. She held on tightly to Susie, and they wept as they shared their pain. Laura thought how terrible it was that Uncle Max remained alive while Aunt Penny was whisked away with so much life still left to live.

EIGHTEEN

It wasn't as she had thought it would be; it wasn't the end either of them had imagined in the slightest, the final ending of such a sweet and loving soul. For Susie, the days after the burial ceremony passed in the slowest manner possible. Laura had invited Susie to stay a few days with them. Susie had lain down on the bed to try to rest, and Laura sat in a chair opposite her. Laura was home, but there was something different about the air now. The difference felt familiar and haunting, and it was beginning to weigh on her.

Eyes glued to the flowers on the wall of her room, with no interest in what was going on around her, Laura sighed and slowly turned her neck just enough to see outside of her window. The day was bright, but behind the brightness, the evening's darkness was approaching. Laura had spent the last four years of her life making a conscientious choice not to be a victim any longer, or at least she thought she had. She tried to build sound, solid walls around her heart to hide her darkness from the world.

She became addicted to learning through the years while navigating the world like every normal person with difficulty. She developed some slight positivity in her life. At least, she had a boyfriend turned best friend and a few great friends. All she focused on now was college and the excitement of the new challenges it would bring. But now, everything just seemed to come crashing back in on her.

If the little-to-no night rest she had was anything to go by, she was sure her demons had come knocking on the door again and in numbers that were about to become too large to bear. The images of Aunt Penny in her coffin made her heart stiffen, and the thoughts of all she had endured made her nights impossible to sleep through.

Mumbling to herself through the night, Laura couldn't help but think, *Why did it have to be Aunt Penny, Uncle Max certainly wouldn't be missed, so why couldn't it have been him?*

Susie needed her mother more than ever as her daily shield and protector. However, it was more complicated now because she would be starting college soon. Laura needed answers as to why life had chosen to cheat her whenever she needed something from it. It felt odd and somewhat bizarre, but the fact she couldn't seem to get the death she craved for every single night her Uncle Max tormented and violated both her body and soul felt strange and made her feel undeserving of life's mercies. Grabbing air in her fists and tightening her hands into balls, Laura bowed her head gently and felt Susie rolling around the bed. Susie was restless, understandably so, for she was certainly missing her mother.

I don't deserve this! Laura whispered to herself. *Susie doesn't deserve any of this either!*

The past few years of high school had passed without too much emotional turmoil and disheartening experiences. Laura had managed to bury her demons beneath a thin, emotionally protective layer, now being gnawed at aggressively as the pent-up emotions fought for release in any way they could.

"Laura!" Susie said as she rubbed her eyes and slowly sat up.

With huge bags underneath each eye and barely able to let her words out, Susie reached for her cousin's hand and slipped her fingers into it. They both shared a sullen and rather pained stare, which held so many unsaid words. They worried spilling any of those words might cause them both to break down uncontrollably.

"I saw her last night," Susie whispered. "I… I saw her."

Laura wished she could soothe her cousin's heart by telling her all she saw was what she needed to see. Susie's mind was doing its best to remember Aunt

Penny as she was before she became ill. She needed to hold onto that loving, healthy, vibrant image of her.

"She is in a better place now," Laura said. "She is in a better place without suffering or pain. She has found peace." But, as the words came from her lips, she couldn't help seeing a Hallmark greeting card flash before her.

Susie slowly retracted her hand and began to shake her head. Susie's distraught state made Laura question whether she ought to have mentioned those words.

"A *better* place?" Susie asked sarcastically as she snapped. "You think she's gone to a better place and decided to leave me here in this world alone?"

The question warranted an answer, not one with words but that of silence, and Laura granted it to her. She wished Susie would simply relax and try to fall back to sleep where she could spend the next few hours in silence and try hard to deal with the thoughts in her own head.

"Mom was kind, and you know it!" Susie's voice grew louder. "She was thoughtful and loving and nice and... and... she's gone!"

Susie was right about Aunt Penny. She was loving and kind, even while she might not have been strong enough to deal with her evil husband properly. Even if she genuinely didn't know about his most heinous crimes, Laura was sure he committed plenty of awful acts against Aunt Penny herself.

"I want to see her again," Susie demanded as she rolled over on the bed.

Laura felt numb as she wondered how to handle her cousin's grief as well as her own. She decided to remain silent. She clenched her fists and steadied her breath. Susie waited for a response but soon realized Laura wasn't going to give her one.

Susie rolled over and accidentally let out a loud ripping noise that sounded deafening in the silence. Laura immediately started laughing and snorted, "Another asshole talking shit!" The girls spiraled into laughter just at the right time. It was good to laugh, even for small moments. The sadness of the past few days was too heavy to bear.

"I'm sorry, Laura." Susie drew closer as she spoke.

Laura shook her head and tried to play down her sadness. "She was completely awesome, and she is gone. She was your mother."

Susie wrapped her arms around Laura gently, and they both shared the moment in silence until Susie burst into tears again.

"I'm going to miss her," she whispered.

Laura felt the same way too, but there was something else she felt swirling within her that she wasn't going to let out. There was a sudden realization that she alone might not be the only victim her Aunt Penny had left alive and unprotected, and that fact made her stomach sink. Susie would have to contend with living in the same house as the man not fit to be called a father or even awarded any form of acknowledgment as a decent human being. Laura had often wondered about Susie's relationship with her father but always stifled it with the same thought. *Surely, he wouldn't do that to his daughter, but what if...maybe it is time to tell. Perhaps it was too long ago and it's better to leave it unsaid.*

"You can stay here for as long as you need to," Laura said to her cousin.

Susie had asked to stay for a few days with them, and Laura could not help but wonder if Uncle Max was part of the reason.

"I don't want to go home," Susie reiterated her desire to stay again. "Everything in there reminds me of her and...."

Laura felt the pause in Susie's tone; it was reminiscent of how she reacted when she wanted to share something but didn't because she thought others might not be able to understand.

Gently easing from Susie's hug and staring into her tear-streaked eyes, which now paled in comparison to the sparkly bright ones she used to have, Laura placed a finger to the girl's lips and smiled.

"You can stay here as long as you want. My mom will be more than willing to have you here."

A word of confirmation came from just inside the door, "Yes, you're welcome to stay as long as you'd like, darling."

Samantha had gone unnoticed by the girls. Laura wondered how long her mother had been standing there, holding a tissue in her hand, and trying to hold back her tears.

"I'm really sorry for you, sweetie." Samantha opened her arms wide and invited Susie over.

Laura let go of her cousin and watched the girl, desperately craving for some maternal comfort, run into Samantha's arms as they shared a warm embrace that lasted for what seemed like forever.

"Penny will always be in our hearts," Samantha said. "She is a part of you, and every time I look at you, I see that wonderful smile of hers in your eyes."

Susie burst into more tears and tightened her arms around Samantha's waist again, Laura joined in the embrace, and the three had a moment of silence in remembrance of Aunt Penny.

"We need to go now, honey," Samantha said.

Somewhat fearful of the answer, Laura stared at her mother and asked, "Where are we going?"

Samantha shrugged and ushered both girls out of the room. It had been the first time in two days since the funeral they were stepping outside, and she felt they needed the air.

"I know it's been tough, and you'd rather stay in your room for the next year, if possible, but two days in there will only make things worse," she explained. "We'll grieve together as a family to remember what a great woman Penny was."

Laura smiled at her mother and halted when she caught sight of the two men sitting in the living room. Emptied beer bottles stood before Uncle Max while Paul sat with his chin placed into his knuckles as he pivoted his hand on his knee with his elbows.

What is this fucking bastard doing here? Laura fought the urge to let the words out.

He sat with an almost empty beer bottle in his hand and barely looked away from the TV as they approached.

"Max," Samantha called to him.

He looked over at the three of them as they came down the hallway. Laura didn't notice any pain in his eyes. Although she knew he was evil, she had assumed there would be some sadness inside him. Laura and her mother walked past him and headed right for the living room with Susie by their side.

"Susie," he called out calmly while gently placing the empty bottle on the table to turn to his daughter.

"I want you to come home," he muttered.

Laura frowned and caught the displeased and unwilling look on her cousin's face. Susie moved her lips as though she had things to say but stopped and took another look in Laura's direction. It became apparent to Laura that her cousin was drained of strength to fight or exert her will. The girl struggled to communicate what she wanted as her thoughts and emotions were mounting up within her.

"She wants to stay here!" Laura said aloud without realizing that she summoned the courage to speak for her cousin.

Uncle Max looked her way, but Laura had managed to look down and tried hard not to make any form of eye contact with him. Everything about him reeked of discomfort for her and would only translate into anger should she decide to look at him for long.

Laura could tell he wanted Susie to hop right into his prized Trans Am and ride home with her. She could tell he wanted to simply yank her by her arms and lead her out the door, but that wasn't possible where he was. He wasn't in his old house where he called the shots and ran around like there were no rules or like other people's emotions didn't matter.

Standing her ground felt good for Laura, even if it wasn't for herself. There was a twinge of sweetness in her confidence, and she hoped to savor it as long as possible. Samantha, ever so instinctive, stared at Laura oddly but wasn't going to demand an explanation right then. She would do it later.

"Is this what you want?" Uncle Max finally asked his daughter.

Susie took her time, but her head finally nodded, even if her voice deserted her. The nod was perfect enough.

Samantha cut in immediately after clearing her throat. "Max, I didn't want to interrupt or tell you what you should do, but the girls have been talking about spending time together here for a bit, it is fine for Susie to stay with us for a while."

Laura watched her father nod his head and reach for Uncle Max's back with a supportive tap as the room fell oddly silent once again.

"If that is what she wants, then she can stay," Uncle Max finally concluded with a loud sigh.

Laura felt the urge to dance swell within her, but that wouldn't be the right move to make under the circumstances.

"I have to pick up some documents at the funeral home, and I'll be heading home from there," he explained as he stood up and reached for his beer to savor the last drop.

Laura shook her head and wondered just how addicted he was and how much longer his liver would last. Crippling thoughts of how the world would be a better place should he get too drunk behind the wheel and decide to ram himself head-on into a pole or ditch. These thoughts quenched the anger-parched beds of her mind as she watched him pull Susie closer and plant a kiss on her forehead.

"Be strong," he whispered while holding her face in his hands.

Barely able to breathe, Susie nodded her head. She seemed to let out a loud sigh in relief when he let go of her and headed for the door. Laura could not help but feel relieved as well.

Good riddance, Laura thought and walked over to Susie who laid her head to rest on Laura's shoulder.

"I still want to see her… I want to…," Susie whispered as she burst into tears.

Laura looked at her father and said nothing, but the man had picked up on what his niece wanted.

"We'll all go for a ride and check out the beautiful changing leaves," he said with a resigned voice.

Samantha agreed with a nod and walked away to get the car keys.

Susie stayed with them for a little more than a week. They supported her the best they could, but Susie needed to figure out how she was going to live without her mother.

NINETEEN

Graduation

High school had been the new beginning that Laura needed. She took the opportunity to reinvent herself. And re-invent herself she did. Working hard in her classes through all four years, she wanted to give her best in everything that she did. She participated in intramural swimming and diving. She thought it was awesome that her small private school had a pool. Growing up with a pool in her backyard, she enjoyed the water and felt at home there. At the beginning of high school, she made a point to be friends with everyone and friends with no one at the same time. Laura didn't want anyone knowing who she really was on the inside. As she worked to get good grades, she showed only the side of her that she wanted people to see.

Sitting in the library, pen in hand, staring at her paper, she was lost in thought. In just a few short days, she would have to give a speech to the entire graduating class and everyone attending the ceremony. She didn't set out to be the valedictorian. As a matter of fact, she wasn't even paying attention to anyone else's GPA. She had focused only on her grades, how well she could do, and did her best to earn a college scholarship. Ideally, to a school far away, maybe somewhere south. Laura had visited South Carolina one time with a friend, and she loved the warm air and the white sandy shores, or beaches as they are called in the south. She was ready to leave home and the memories that lived there.

She could recall sitting in pre-calculus when the announcement came over the loudspeaker, "Congratulations to Laura Christine Shirk Senior Class Valedictorian," the student body president said. Laura was shocked. She had no idea she was first in her class, and she had no desire to speak in front of her peers. But giving a speech was the custom, and she had no choice.

Tapping her pen on the table, she sat listening to the second hand on the clock tick and she began to reminisce. The school was small and didn't have cliques. Laura genuinely enjoyed her four years in high school and couldn't believe it was coming to an end. She eventually had bonded with a few girls whom she did allow to get to know her a little better. They were the most unlikely group of friends, each with unique interests and hobbies, none of them alike. Mandy and Casey would smoke weed each morning before school. Kelsie was constantly talking about sex, having sex, getting sex, loving sex, hating sex, sex, sex, sex. Then there was Jenny, the sweetest girl you would ever meet. Laura, thinking about her past four years, chuckled as she chewed on her pen.

As a freshman, she began searching for who she was. She wanted to be anything other than the little girl whom her Uncle Max molested. She wanted to be more, so she chose to do everything she did to the absolute best of her ability. In her mind, the better person she could become, the wiser person she could become, the more she could learn the more understanding she could be, then the more she could be forgiven for her sins of the past. In her mind, she still blamed herself. She had years to tell herself everything she could have done differently to avoid her Uncle Max's atrocities. Laura wanted to "best" herself into forgiveness.

Now, as a senior, she felt much stronger and more confident. As her eyes scanned the library with twenty or so students in it, she remembered getting into a fistfight in the cafeteria back in 1992. At that moment, she decided she would always stand up for herself and others if needed. It was then that everyone else learned that Laura wouldn't take shit from anyone. She sat thinking about the incident…

When the lunch bell rang, the students raced to the cafeteria. Just like every other high school in America, everyone sat in the same seats during lunch. One sly girl, named Ann, who had a crush on Laura's boyfriend thought she would get everyone to move to a different table, leaving Laura to sit alone. Ann was disappointed to find out when she arrived at the "new" table no one had obliged. Laura wasn't sure if anyone actually took her side or if they thought the whole thing was stupid and felt it best to sit in their usual seats. Either way, Ann was furious and began screaming, "You are such a bitch, I hate you. You have everything, and you parade around here like you are God's gift to everyone. I'm going to kill you!" And BAM, a Snickers bar whacked Laura square in the head. She hadn't even noticed Ann throwing it at her.

"That's it. I've had enough. You've been treating me like shit since I got to this school. I don't know what I've done, but I've had enough," Laura shouted. With that, she leaped onto the table and ran along its top to where Ann was standing. Laura didn't know what came over her, but she decided to take a stand at that moment on that day. Lunging at Ann, she jumped off the table and struck her as many times as she could with both fists. Ann was pulling Laura's hair and tried to kick and claw at her. Laura grabbed Ann by the shoulders to hold her like a target and began kneeing her in the stomach.

"Girls, girls, GIRLS...stop this right now," Sister Maria yelled. She stepped in between the two students *pushing them apart. "Both of you to the principal's office now!"*

With the light now gleaming through the decorated stain glass window of the library, Laura smiled at the many memories she had in this place. The good and the bad, each having its own lesson rolled up inside. But she was not a writer, and she was not one to be on stage. So, what words could she possibly put together that would inspire her classmates?

"Hey, Laura, what are you working on?" Mrs. Charles said.

Mrs. Charles was her English teacher. She was a round woman, and she always wore long dresses, more like frocks. Her hair was brown with a slight reddish tint and very unruly. She wore makeup, but in all the wrong shades that made her look a little like a clown.

"Hi, I'm trying to write my valedictorian speech," Laura mumbled, defeated. "I'm not having much luck."

The teacher sat beside her and offered to help. For a moment, Laura was relieved because she had no idea where to even begin.

"You know most valedictorians think they have accomplished something by being first in their class, but in my experience, they go off to college and don't amount to anything," Mrs. Charles said. Laura was confused by this statement.

***

It was a warm June day, perfect for her graduation. She could see her parents in the audience and sitting next to them were Matthew and Mary. They were smiling and so proud. Her stomach was in knots, the nerves almost too much to bear. The ceremony began with the traditional tune of "Pomp and Circumstance" as the graduates walked down the aisle to their seats in the front of the room. Laura's seat was on the stage, along with the salutatorian, the student body government, and a few other students and teachers. Sitting in her seat and squirming side to side, Laura waited for the dreaded moment.

She moved the microphone down closer to her lips as she prepared to speak. Looking at the teacher who just introduced her, she began, "Good evening, thank you, Sister Maria. Thank you, students, teachers, parents, and staff, all of you have had such a positive impact on me during the last four years. It is my greatest honor to speak here today."

Lies, she thought, *I'd rather have my nails plucked from my fingers.*

"I stand here before you and I reflect on the great moments of the past and the great moments still to come. None of us know what lies ahead, but we know that we are prepared to accept whatever might come our way. This school has helped to mold strong young women who will surely be your leaders for tomorrow. You have taught us to be confident yet humble, bold yet gentle, searching for greatness yet grateful."

The middle was fuzzy, and Laura thought she might pass out, but doing her best to read the words she had typed on her pages and flipping to the last page, she continued.

"As we embark on our journey of life, remember the words of Mother Teresa."

People are often unreasonable and self-centered. Forgive them anyway.

If you are kind, people may accuse you of ulterior motives. Be kind anyway.

If you are honest, people may cheat you. Be honest anyway.

If you find happiness, people may be jealous. Be happy anyway.

Give the world the best you have, and it may never be enough. Give your best anyway.

"We will get what we give to this world, so let's give it our ALL."

Lifting her fist and pumping it in the air, Laura shouted, "I love you, class of 1994. Let's go forth and conquer!" The audience began clapping, and the students were cheering and shouting. Samantha and Paul were beaming so brightly it was almost blinding.

***

Laura was feeling a mix of emotions post-graduation. She was excited to take on the next chapter of her life, ready to be eight hours away from home and embarking on new adventures. Yet, despite her excitement, she couldn't help but feel twisted inside her gut about Susie. She missed her Aunt Penny, but she worried about Susie even more. She couldn't bear the thought of moving such a long distance away and not telling a single soul about Uncle Max. The traumatic events she lived through had found some resting place in the deep dark corners of her mind. *Could she really bring them back to the surface again?* The nagging question remained. *What if he was hurting Susie?*

After tormenting her mind with questions and fear for several days, she decided that it was indeed time. Deciding it was time was one thing but speaking the words into existence was another thing entirely. However, Laura remained determined in her decision. Afraid she would lose her courage, she searched the house frantically for her mother. Finally spotting her in

214

the backyard watering the garden, she pushed open the glass door and called for Samantha.

Waving her arms, she yelled, "Mom," as she closed the door and began walking toward her mother.

"Mom, I have something that I need to tell you. I really must talk to you now. I'll help you finish up, and then, can we sit and talk?"

Samantha looked oddly at her daughter, the garden hose in hand still watering the tomato plants in front of her. "Sure. Actually, I'm just finishing up. Let me put the hose away, and we can talk. Is everything ok?"

"Yes, everything's okay. I just need to talk to you. I need to do it now, before I lose my courage." Samantha was starting to get a little nervous. She had no idea what Laura wanted to tell her, but she could sense it was important.

"Okay, Laura. Let's go sit by the pool and we can chat. I'll put the hose away later."

"Thanks…okay…well, I don't really know how to begin," Laura was squirming in her seat now. She hadn't thought about how she was going to say the words.

"Laura honey, whatever it is, it's okay. You can talk to me."

Sucking in what felt like all the air around her, Laura took a long deep breath and exhaled slowly. "Mom, before I start, I need you to understand that I am ok. I need you to listen and don't say anything until I finish so that I can get through this."

Samantha was sitting up a little straighter now, "Okay, Laura, I'm listening. I love you, and I'm here for you no matter what this is about." Inside, she was terrified, hoping her daughter would hurry up and spill her words so she could deal with whatever was coming.

Laura decided there was no easy way to break the news, so she just came out with it, "Do you remember when I tried to tell you and Dad that Uncle Max kissed me?"

Samantha nodded her head slowly, "Yes, I remember."

"Well, he didn't actually kiss me. He did colossally worse. He did unspeakable things to me. I'm sorry, Mom. I didn't know how to tell you, and I thought you'd be angry. I thought I'd done something wrong. I was young and confused, and I didn't understand."

Samantha opened her mouth to speak but decided to reach for her daughter's hand instead. Feeling the warmth of her mother's hand, Laura began to weep gently, her tears slowly streaming down her face. "Mom, I'm telling you this now because I'm leaving for school, and I felt like you needed to know. I don't want to relive those moments, so I need you to understand and respect that. I'm begging you not to make me do anything with this information. Just keep an eye on Susie and make sure she's doing ok."

The two sat and talked for hours. Laura felt even closer to her mother now that she shared her burden. Samantha was strong, and Laura imagined that she must have had so many questions, so much anger towards Uncle Max, so many emotions, but she remained calm and resolute as she listened to her daughter. She consoled her, reassured her, and loved her. It was a good step for Laura. She still had quite a bit of healing to do, but she could see and feel the light building back inside her.

***

Standing in their living room, the family knew the time had come to say goodbye. It seemed only a day since they had handed Laura her diploma, but August was upon them, and it was time to go to college. Laura had suffered silently for most of her life. She still had plenty of invisible scars, and she had enough to work through in her head. To Laura, new challenges were exciting, and she would take each opportunity to start new and re-invent herself whenever she could. Through each transformation, she was stronger, wiser, and more confident. She loved her family dearly, but she couldn't stay. Laura needed to escape from this town and everything it reminded her of. She needed to find herself, to become someone she could love. Sniffling gently, Samantha was in the kitchen packing up some snacks. Laura could see small tears rolling down her mom's cheeks.

"Mom, don't cry. I'm only going eight hours away, and I'll be back in a few months for fall break."

Samantha put her arms around her daughter, and speaking softly, she said "No, my girl, this is it. I can feel it in my heart. You might be back to visit, but you'll never be back for good." She pinched Laura's nose and then gave her an even bigger squeeze.

Waving as she drove away from her childhood stucco house with the steel gate that offered her protection, Laura turned up the music in her teal green Ford Mustang and headed for her next adventure. College was the next step on her journey to finding herself and overcoming her demons.

TWENTY

Fall 1994

S tanding there silently, Laura took in her dorm room. She felt free, far away from her past and the secrets she had been keeping. Filled with a mixture of emotions she was elated to begin her new journey at Methodist University.

The walls of the room were made of cinder blocks and painted a light tan, almost white. Somehow, she lucked out with her rooming assignment and was given a room in the nicer dorm. Most first-year students had to stay in the freshmen dorm, with community showers and furniture that was probably 100 years old. Laura, however, was grateful for her new domain. The dorm had been built only three years earlier, so everything was still practically brand new. There were two twin-size beds, two matching wooden desks with matching chairs, and two matching wardrobes—almost indestructible typical dorm room furniture.

"Hi!" Laura heard a voice from behind that startled her. Charging at her to give her a big hug was Laura's roommate, Chaney. Laura, caught off guard, jumped back. Bursting into laughter, the girls embraced.

"Hi, Chaney! I wasn't sure if you'd be here yet."

"I got here a little while ago," Chaney replied.

Chaney was super nice and provided a little piece of home, for she grew up in Laura's hometown. Although the girls never went to school or played sports together, they did somewhat know each other. It was nice to know that a tiny piece of home was on campus with her, even better, a piece that didn't truly know Laura.

The girls began unpacking; Laura decorated her side of the room in Mickey Mouse. She loved Disney and insisted that her new college dorm room bedspread be Mickey Mouse with matching sheets. She brought a Mickey Mouse TV with a built-in VCR and a Mickey Mouse phone. Chaney worked her way around her side of the room and hung pictures of friends and posters of fitness supermodels all over the walls. Chaney was insanely fit, chiseled in all the right places, but not too much. She still had a feminine physique. Her brown hair was long and soft, and twisted up into a French braid.

"Laura, what are you doing," Chaney shouted from inside the dorm room. Laura had moved on to the bathroom that they shared. Two dorm rooms were connected to a bathroom to make a suite. It was much nicer than having to share a bathroom with an entire floor of freshman girls.

"I'm in the bathroom. I got a new shower curtain to hang in here," Laura said.

Chaney laughed and rolled her eyes. "Of course, you did. You brought everything for the room and then some."

"Well, I didn't want to leave it open. Water could get everywhere."

"Yeah, good idea. Ugg, what is that smell?" Chaney asked.

"I think it might be the shower curtain. It smells pretty gross in here. Maybe we can open a window and air it out. I think I'm mostly unpacked. I'm going to lie down, but I'll open the window first."

Chaney was putting the finishing touches on the room while Laura relaxed on her new bed. She lay there thinking about the days ahead, what school would be like, how she might fit in, and she wondered if she would make friends.

Staring up at the ceiling, she thought about how far she had come. She was incredibly grateful for her mother's love and support. Laura still had a lot of work to do in finding herself, but she would accept the challenge in this new environment. College would be different. Laura was different, smarter more capable. She had decided in high school that she would no longer be a follower. Laura wasn't going to do what others wanted her to do just to fit in. Instead, she would make her own decisions. Laura would take responsibility for her actions and be her own person. Yes, she had secrets, some skeletons in her closet, but Laura Shirk knew who she was, and she was ready to start moving forward.

TWENTY-ONE

December 1994

The daunting words continued to bicker in her head like a beating drum, which only spurred her on. By her count, she had gone out on eight dates within the space of a month, but none of those boys mattered; they were all counts and means to a definite end lying deep within her soul. This time around, Laura had decided to push herself a step further.

It might be worth it, she thought to herself as she held the phone in her hand.

She had decided to take a page from the books of other girls, who seemed nonchalant and casual about having sex with guys. Laura fought with herself desperately day and night to muster enough courage to be alone in her room with a guy. Her date just required a phone call and an invitation to go along with it, but the words didn't come as easy as she had thought they would.

Laura had battled various reasons for years. The question regarding why any guy would want to be with her had not entirely gone away. Aunt Penny's death had acted like an enormous-sized sledgehammer plunging hard into the "safety wall" she had hidden everything behind in high school. Finding the courage to tell her mother helped to a small degree, but she still had more demons left to conquer.

"He might not come," she whispered impatiently.

She wandered through thoughts in her troubled mind, and her eyes remained shut as she tried to picture herself finally letting go and allowing any intimacy to occur freely. This particular guy had managed to stick for several weeks now, constantly keeping in touch and showing genuine care. Even if his actions wouldn't matter, she assumed giving him a chance might be worth a try. Mostly, it might be worth it for her and him as well.

Just do it and get it over with, she heard the voice rage loudly in her head, and this time, with some excitement about the demand that made the voice impossible to ignore.

Laura fought hard to block the voice out, but it wouldn't stay suppressed, even with one final failed attempt. She reached for the doorknob, yanked at it gently, and turned it until the air in the hallway slowly invaded her room. Feeling a mix of butterflies coursing through her belly and her heart drumming aloud, she froze momentarily to have a quick rethink.

There he was. Standing and staring at her awkwardly, he awaited her permission to enter her room. Laura barely stared at him or looked into his eyes, but she could feel his staunch gaze of confusion as he stood there, dressed in his faded blue denim jeans and fitted round neck t-shirt that hugged his physique and screamed out the perfection his body carried.

"Laura!" he called out to her, who seemed to have spaced out on him. "Can I come in? I've been standing here for a minute."

Laura finally snapped out of her daze and stepped aside to let him in. She cleared her throat and watched him open his arms to hug her, but she barely tightened hers around him in return.

"Leo." She smiled and waved him to have a seat on her bed.

Leo smiled back and made his way to the edge of the mattress before slipping off his shoes and placing them at the foot of the bed. Laura wondered what would come next. She knew deep inside that the kissing and caressing she had performed over the past weeks meant anything was possible tonight, and the thought scared her.

She wanted the normalcy every other girl her age felt and exuded. Like the other girls in college, she wanted bouncy and bubbly emotions that made them free and willing to indulge in relationships. She wanted "a life" free of past scars, and while her search had brought her nothing but struggle and difficulty, she wasn't going to stop until she found some form of normalcy or, at least, until she was sure normalcy wasn't ever going to be possible for her.

Leo turned and smiled at her again, "Laura, is something going on with you?"

Laura came back into focus and hurried to the bed to cast off any disgruntled impression Leo might begin to have towards her. He had asked her out on a date just a few weeks before, and he seemed genuinely sweet. His dreamy eyes captured her interest from the moment he walked up to her. His smile caused her to laugh uncontrollably too, but … there was always a "but…" and she felt uneasy with him even though she couldn't put her finger on why.

"You want to hang out here instead of my place?" Leo asked.

Laura bobbed her head and smiled. She felt more confident at her place, but that wasn't the sole reason. Her dorm room brought her the feeling of safety she wasn't sure she could ever get anywhere else. Also, unlike spending the night at his apartment, being in her dorm room meant she could control the events and happenings within it.

Leo sat and continued to stare at her as he grew somewhat impatient. Laura had given the entire evening some thought but still had no idea how she was going to survive the night. He was the first boy she ever invited into her room, and while she had turned down many other boys she went out with, Laura had asked for him to come simply because she needed to prove something to herself. Whatever the reason, she remained confused as she stood from the bed and began to pace around the room.

Leo sighed and tilted his head downwards as he rested it into his hand. "I really don't understand what's going here, Laura! You asked me to be here, and now you can barely even speak to me, let alone sit with me?"

Laura gulped down some hard lumps lodged in her throat. Trying hard not to stiffen every muscle in her body and hold her breath too long, she turned to look at him. Leo was handsome, and his perfectly shaped lips and piercing gaze would thrill any girl. However, a question kept echoing in her head while she stood there, staring at the boy she had invited into her dorm room.

What exactly is his end game?

The damaged part of her being had doubted he would want to be with her. In fact, she was hell-bent on him not showing up and would have staked a million dollars on him bailing, but he had surprised her. In doing so, he had managed to remind her she was worthy and someone he would genuinely want to be involved with. However, one significant issue was still tagging along with everything: he was a boy, a male, and a man in entirety. She still struggled to be touched, yet she thought being alone with him was a good idea.

Laura hurried to her bathroom and splashed water on her face. She helped herself to a towel to dry off, and she watched the mild makeup go off as she wiped. Feeling somewhat naked and suddenly more exposed as if a layer of her confidence had worn off, Laura returned to the bedside and sat a short distance from Leo, who was indeed confused.

"Thanks for coming," Laura spoke in a reserved tone.

Leo smiled and responded, "Thanks for inviting me over. I'm looking forward to spending tonight with you."

Laura nodded but fought her natural instincts as he reached over to take her hand into his.

Don't yank your hand out from his, Laura! Don't you dare yank your hand out!

It was the same voice always trying to place her in such situations to toughen her up so she could face her demons. The voice, acting as her guide towards healing, had broken when Aunt Penny passed away. Her inner thoughts had dwelled in her head as though they had never left, and at every turn, they reminded her of how broken she was. They tried to push her towards finding healing through any means, like the uncomfortable situation she put herself in now. However, Laura listened and acted accordingly.

Leo caressed her hand gently and smiled as he hoped he was setting the mood for what would be a lovely night. He eyed Laura like he could not wait to have her. He was oblivious to the crazy thoughts and reservations that were going through Laura's mind. Or at least, if he did notice, they didn't dissuade him in the least.

"I must confess I wasn't sure you'd go out with me, much less ask me to be here tonight," he said.

Finding something to distract herself with, Laura asked, "What do you mean?"

Leo shrugged and took a moment to reply. "I mean, you aren't the easiest girl to be with, or at least that's what I've heard."

Laura froze and felt the need to retract her hand, but she let it remain within his. The truth was his touch on her skin was beginning to make her uncomfortable.

However, she wasn't about to give in to whatever belief he might have in his head about her. Backing out now would only play right into everything he had heard.

Sighing softly and managing a smile as she grew a little bit more comfortable with him, she spoke, "I really don't know what you've heard, but I'm not as difficult as you make me sound."

Leo raised his right brow and smiled before leaning closer to her hand and lifting it halfway until his lips gently cemented themselves on her skin. Laura tensed and felt the hairs on her neck stand. Flashes of "his" lips touching her body were accompanied by the sick feeling it had brought her years ago. Uncle Max slowly crept back into her consciousness, and she hurriedly yanked her hand out from within his grasp.

"Did I do something wrong?" Leo looked up and asked as she slowly got to her feet and walked towards the mirror on her dorm room wall.

Laura shook her head and began rubbing the area his lips had touched. She wished she could hurry into the bathroom and scrub the exact spot clean, but to do so would come off as rude, and she didn't want to be rude.

"I'm sorry," she replied. "You've done nothing wrong, but...."

Leo sneaked up on her and put his arms around her waist as he held her tightly from behind and stared into the mirror with his head resting on her shoulder. Laura could see the glimmer of happiness in his eyes. He seemed to like her, but she could barely think about any such positive emotions considering he was standing "behind" her and holding her tightly.

"Please ... please," she mumbled in a soft tone while his hands moved around her waist and slowly began heading toward her breasts.

Laura closed her eyes and tried to block her mind from those suffocating memories from years past. She was eighteen now and had the right to some emotional freedom, yet she remained that little girl, violated and not allowed to mature past the day the horrifying incident first occurred.

Feeling Leo's touch continue to make her skin crawl and her heart threaten to implode, she turned around and broke his grip around her waist, just as his left hand had almost managed to touch her breast. She still couldn't summon complete breaths, for her heart felt like it would give way, and her lungs with it.

"What is…," a befuddled-looking Leo was about to ask when she stopped him by sinking her lips onto his and forcing her arms around his neck so quickly in order to distract herself. He accepted her lips on his and reached for the back of her neck with his hand as they headed to the bed.

231

Laura thanked the stars, so far, so good. She was doing it. She was allowing herself to be physical with a man, even if her heart felt like it could have a hemorrhage of some sort. Finally, they both landed on the bed, Leo on his back while Laura assumed the position on top of him.

Leo flipped her over and pinned Laura down so he could have unfettered access to her body as he warmed her face with kisses and veered downwards towards her breasts.

"Please!" Laura cried as she fought to get her hands freed. "Please don't ... Please!"

Leo ignored her plea while he pinned her left hand onto the bed. Suddenly, like a wounded lion backed into a corner, Laura roared and shoved him off immediately, snapping her arms free. Breathing heavily, she watched Leo retreat from the bed and stare at her in an incredibly puzzled manner.

Laura parted her lips to speak but clamped them shut as she adjusted her top and sat up.

"I thought you liked me? I mean, I believed we had this connection going on between us for weeks now," Leo said.

Laura wished she could tell him the truth, that whatever connection he felt they had or had been sharing for weeks now was nothing more than a means to an end for her. It was the painful truth and one that could undoubtedly destroy or damage his self-esteem to some degree. But her reaction wasn't about him; it was about Laura and her unresolved demons.

Laura tried to answer him but fell short of words. "I honestly don't think I know," she said.

It was as honest as she could be, for everything about him had begun to spook her from the moment she felt his lips touch her skin. His soft lips were like razors scraping against her tender skin, and his breath felt like hot lava crawling along her neck when he kissed her.

Sighing aloud and crawling out of bed, she turned and stared at him blankly. "Can we call it a night, please?"

Not knowing what to say, Leo simply nodded his head and reached for one of the pillows on the bed.

Laura held a finger up and shook her head, "Sorry, but if you're going to stay, you'll have to sleep on the floor."

Seeing him obey her command by stepping away from the bed and finding himself a comfortable spot on the concrete floor was strange, but the command brought her some control. Her entire body embraced this empowerment over him, even if he wasn't the one to wrong or scar her.

The control felt good, and Laura sighed in relief, but even at that, she could not repel the darkness swelling within her. She could see Uncle Max's face smirking in her memories and feel his touch taunting at her skin from beyond time as she crawled into bed and wrapped herself tightly with her comforter.

Leo, cold and without the warm affection he had craved from the cold-hearted girl lying in bed just a few feet from him, whispered, "If I did anything wrong, I'm truly sorry."

The words sent streams of hurt mixed with guilt down Laura's spine. She realized he had done nothing wrong other than show his affection for her. He had not been there years ago when the devil came knocking on her door, and he bore no relation with her Uncle Max, other than the fact he was a male, as was the man she could never rid herself of psychologically.

"I'm sorry too," she whispered, but so low that only she could hear.

Laura closed her eyes and felt her soul unleash so much guilt mixed with anger that translated into burning tears rolling down her cheeks. Laura had come to realize the feeling that she could not allow herself to be loved still remained within her. She hoped there was the possibility she could allow herself to be liked by a select few men such as Leo. She didn't find herself worthy of such affection, and they certainly didn't deserve the level of crazy she was going to dish out.

Broken and struggling, she let the familiar tears drown her to sleep. College was supposed to be different; however, she had left her comfort zone to be miles away from her support, her family. The distance was another way of pushing herself, but Uncle Max was there regardless, a part of her being, a voyager in her soul an unwanted third party in her encounters.

For Leo, who slept on the floor in silence and wished the morning sun would come quickly enough, he would take to his heels and never look back. It would be the last meeting between the two and his final attempt to break through whatever walls she had up and around her. Many men like him were bound to take the same step.

Laura could only hope one would be strong yet gentle enough to break down those walls. But, even so, she assumed her fortress would never come down, at least, not in her lifetime.

TWENTY-TWO

May 1995

The loud cheers from those supporting their respective volleyball-playing friends rang out and startled Laura, and she, in turn, stood up with her hands clapping wildly. The sun was shining brightly, and many of the students enjoyed hanging by the courts in their bathing suits and soaking up the rays while the guys played.

"Come on, Leo!" she cried atop her voice and sighed when she realized he wasn't even looking her way.

She watched the bare-chested men knock the ball around while ladies roared their names and jumped up and down. The air was hot and stale, but school was done for the day, and it was time to play. Like Coppertone models, all the girls sat around the beach courts slathering sunscreen on their legs with their toes pointed forward as they smiled and giggled at the boys at play.

The girls to her right screamed aloud once again for Leo, the same person she had come to watch. Hearing them cheer for him caused a stir of discomfort within her as she shrugged and got to her feet.

She realized she would rather be in her dorm room than watch other girls cheer on her ex-boyfriend or whatever they had going on before it ended some months back. In all fairness, Laura recognized Leo had done his best, but Laura had done even better in making sure she wasn't accessible emotionally. Furthermore, she had been asked out by most of the boys currently on the court. One by one, Laura either turned them down or went out on one date and tossed them away like yesterday's trash.

Looking away, Laura caught sight of another college boy she had a thing with that barely lasted a week. The thought of how many boys she had gone on dates with hit her like a brick. Laura felt sad for them. She was a predator, and they were her prey. They couldn't know how hollowed out she was or how tall and thick her walls were.

"Hello to you too, Daniel," she mumbled to herself as she watched him walk past her at a quickened pace.

Laura rolled her eyes, picked up her bag, and slapped it over her shoulder before taking the first few steps towards the dormitory where she hoped a nice shower and some rest would help clear her head.

"Leaving so soon?" an unfamiliar voice called without mentioning her name, but Laura could sense he was talking to her.

Somewhat tired and assuring herself she wasn't going to indulge any creep of a boy who might be trying to get her attention, she remained with her gaze up ahead, and her demeanor showed no signs of wanting to turn around.

Without looking back, she asked, "What's it to ya?"

She heard the fellow grumble and clear his throat. "Well, if my former roommate's girlfriend is leaving the game early, then I guess I should ask why."

"Confident" was the word she could use to describe the way he spoke. Considering the only guy on campus she had dated longer than one week was Leo, she assumed she was talking to Leo's old roommate. However, she remembered he had long curly red hair that didn't interest Laura, but Leo spoke well of him most of the time. Laura felt torn between simply walking away or engaging him in a conversation.

Laura decided to indulge him in conversation, but she wasn't entirely sure why. Standing topless and glistening in the sun with sweat mixed with sand from playing beach volleyball, he grinned back at her wildly as he swung his shirt over his shoulder.

"You must be Tom," Laura said in a tone indicating she wasn't in any way interested in engaging him for too long.

He smiled, reached out his hand, and replied, "And you're Laura. I'm glad you've heard of me."

His confidence level continued to heighten, and his cockiness was apparent as well. Laura took a moment to gawk at the young man before her eyes. Drawing attention to his bright blue eyes, she noticed that he had cut his hair, and she took in his perfect physique. He was one of those outspoken, irresistible jocks who had the charm to choose any girl he wanted.

"Well, it's nice officially meeting you, Tom. You cut your hair, I see." She managed a teasing smile but left his out-stretched hand hanging as she turned around and began walking away.

Tom made no move to follow her. He slowly withdrew his hand, stood there, and watched Laura walk away in her blue and white striped bikini.

Laura paused and turned around before saying, "By the way, Leo and I aren't a thing any longer. We ended it a while back. We kind of weren't a real thing anyway, but we're still good friends. Oh, and, I have sand all over me, so that's why I'm leaving early, since you asked."

Tom nodded and watched Laura turn around again as she walked away. He raced after her, and with his arms spread apart, he blocked her path to the main sidewalk leading to the dormitory. Taking in her perfect curves, he shook his head and stared at Laura up and down while Laura simply continued to stand there and stare back at him.

"Leo wouldn't know a good thing if it hit him in the face," Tom finally blurted out.

Her expression not changing, Laura managed to shrug.

"It's all good. We're better as friends. Unfortunately, he couldn't handle me," she replied with a smug look before maneuvering her way around him.

Mumbling to himself, Tom remained glued to the spot for a while as Laura walked on ahead. She could feel his eyes pinned on her back and her butt as he allowed himself a lengthy view before racing to catch up with her once again.

"I'm truly sorry for his loss," he said.

Laura yawned and replied, "Like I said, he couldn't handle me. I'm a tough cookie."

Tom gently held her back by her shoulder, causing Laura to stop, but surprisingly, she did not squirm by the touch of his hand.

"What do you mean he couldn't handle you? Are you sure it wasn't the other way around?"

Laura shrugged and managed a smile.

"I'm guessing you've been meeting a whole lot of wrong dudes. I mean, how difficult can it be? I bet I'd handle you just fine if you were with me," he said with a little glimmer in his eye and some mischief in his smile.

Laura added "Flirtatious" to his list of attributes and began walking away from him. She wasn't interested, but she had to admit he had a way about him.

He remained rooted to the spot this time and voiced loudly, "I guess you're the one chickening out now, aren't you?"

Laura paused, took in a deep breath, and turned back around while she searched her bag for paper. Then, taking out her notepad, she scribbled her dorm room phone number onto it and handed it to Tom. "Trust me, you should save yourself some time and sanity by leaving me alone."

"I guess I'll see you later, Laura," he shouted as they parted ways. She was impressed he remembered her name since she hadn't written it down with her number.

Hoping to put thoughts of the boy out of her mind and have a good shower before heading to the cafeteria for dinner, Laura simply waved him off and headed for her room.

***

Barely stepping into her dorm room, the phone rang aloud and grabbed her attention as she hurried over to answer it.

"Hello, Laura," the now familiar voice said.

Laura felt her face redden and her lips curl into a smirk as she wondered if giving him her phone number was a good idea. However, she couldn't ignore the tingle she felt at the sound of his voice on the other end of the phone. She was shocked by butterflies, but she couldn't deny it.

"What do you want, Tom?" she asked outright with her hand on her hip and her eyes rolling at the wall.

Tom took no time to give his response. He barely hesitated or took a breath before he answered, "A shower with you."

Laura took the phone from her left ear and switched it to her right as she wondered if she had heard correctly.

"You heard me, Laura. Come and have a shower with me. We're both sweaty and dirty from the court. I know I need a shower, don't you? You even said you were sandy. So, come and keep me company".

His boldness completely amazed her, and even more, the fact that he didn't hold back in any way.

"Are you chicken?" he teased on and tried to provoke a response from her. "Does this mean you're too scared to accept my offer?"

Laura remained silent and unsure of what to make of the daunting boy. He was obviously trying to taunt her into accepting his offer, and regardless of how forward the request might be, he was willing to have it happen. They weren't good friends, and they certainly weren't close enough for her to go to his dorm, much less take a shower in his bathroom.

Her heart raced wildly with this new dilemma, as she held the phone to her ear. Tightening her fist around the phone, she slammed it back into the cradle and walked away. She was tempted to prove herself capable of a shower with another human, another test for herself. She thought of the prospect of being with a man in the bathroom, but with those memories, she assumed that she would never want that to happen again.

Her reckless side encouraged her to give him a shot while the never-forgiving part of her paced around the room and shook her head. Making the decision was hard because she had never done something as daring as taking a shower with a guy before. Laura stared at the phone long and hard before looking at her own body, which was indeed in need of a shower.

"Screw it," she whispered and marched over to the phone to dial back the number that had just called her.

***

Tom was frantically running around his room collecting the dirty clothes lying around, so he could organize them in a pile behind the couch in the middle of the room. He had always felt like he was the nice guy. But nice guys finish last. He had recently broken up with a girl because she cheated on him. He was tired of being Mister Nice Guy. Tom thought that Laura was smoking hot, and there was something about her that made him wild inside.

Normally, he wouldn't have had the courage even to say hello, let alone have a conversation with her, much less ask her to come over for a shower. So, what on earth was he thinking? Tom was having a mini freak-out moment, but he couldn't back out now. Laura Shirk, the girl every dude on campus wanted to conquer, and very few were able to get her attention, was coming over to his room.

Who was he kidding? He was a nice guy. He had a moment when he wanted to be the guy who didn't care about the girl; he wanted to have his way and then dump her like so many guys do. The bad guys are always the ones that get the girl. His heart was racing, and he didn't know what to do. He hadn't imagined that she would say yes! But he couldn't back down now—not this time.

***

Standing in the doorway with her heart almost in her throat and her knees practically turning to jelly, Laura recounted her decision as she reached for the door. Staring at the familiar dormitory door and wondering if she were placing herself in a situation she would come to regret, her heart had stopped then and there. Although having regrets for placing herself in uncomfortable situations wasn't her thing, joining him in the shower felt different. Her relationship with Tom at this point was practically non-existent, and she had no tale to tell about him if she were asked. Yet there was something about him and the way he had asked her to come shower with him that intrigued her.

He had done it without any nervousness in his voice, and she could feel his confidence daring her as best as he could. He was without a doubt a handsome fellow with an amazing body, but he was practically a stranger. Finally, with a subtle sigh of exhaustion mentally and physically, Laura mumbled to herself, *It's just a shower.*

You can show him who's boss and get the hell out of there once you're done.

The words barely brought any strength to her weakened knees as she remained just outside the front door of his dorm and felt helpless. Laura's memories continued to play images of her most horrifying shower with Uncle Max in a continuous loop in her head. Battling the images as she walked through the lobby approaching his door, Laura shook her head furiously.

She reached for the door and clenched her hand into a fist so that she could announce her arrival. Instead, the door slowly gave way with a creaking noise that indicated it had been left open. Perplexed and puzzled but without moving from her spot, Laura felt her thoughts go haywire as she tried to figure out what was going on.

Did he leave the door open?

The lights in the room were on, and she could see his flip-flops just past the door inside the room, indicating he had been in the room and was most likely still in there. Heart pounding and mind racing with different scenarios and possibilities, she finally broke her knees free of the stiffness they felt and took the first step halfway into the room.

You can do it, she continued to recite in her head.

She needed to be free from her past. She needed to move forward. She needed to shed her invisible scars. She wondered if stepping into the shower with another man would find a way of erasing the impact the boogie man had left in her subconscious. Laura wanted to get into the shower, but the "ifs" were piling up and could come at a dangerous price the more she thought of joining him.

It's just a shower; she tried convincing herself again as she entered the room and stood a few feet from the door.

The door slowly swung shut and back into position with the assistance of the wind, which gave Laura the jitters. Watching it slam shut unsettled her heart and almost caused her to panic as she gulped the accumulated saliva and nervousness down her throat. However, something else made her even more nervous, and it came in the form of the humming voice she could hear from the bathroom.

Tom was already in the shower doing his thing; he didn't wait for her. She realized maybe the door was left open by accident, and perhaps he wasn't expecting her at all. On the other hand, maybe the door was left open as an invitation for her to come in. Either way, entering was her choice.

He must be crazy, but I did warn him that he didn't know what he was getting himself into.

***

In the shower, the water was beating down his face, Tom decided he didn't know what to do, so he just hopped in. He figured if Laura came, she could decide what she wanted to do, and if she didn't come, he would still have his shower. As he listened for Laura, Tom's heart pounded rapidly in his chest.

Laura heard the shower stream hitting the floor. She cringed within and felt her bag drop from her hand. Her heart kicked and screamed for her to run, but she pushed ahead foolishly challenging herself. In fact, challenging was all she did, defy the sanity of her heart and go with whatever crazy ideas and thoughts that graced the fields of her battered mind.

Laura slowly pulled off her tank top. She felt her body cry for strength as her hands yanked the top over her head and she laid it neatly on his bed. She felt the sting of reality brush her sensitive skin as she began taking off her bikini as well. Standing naked in his room was nothing short of surreal. By this time, her raging heart had given up, ready to stop beating and ultimately on the verge of a panic attack as she crossed the threshold into his bathroom.

Just a step further, she told herself with each step closer toward the shower door.

"Tom," she whispered as she stepped into the shower and felt her organs collapse inside her chest.

Tom remained with his back turned to her, while Laura admired his large calves, which stood in full view right in front of her.

Twenty-Three

The air thinned between them as Laura stared at the man with curious eyes. Tom slowly turned around to look at her. She had imagined the first look he'd have on his face when he realized she had indeed taken up his dare and challenged him by stepping into the shower. For Laura, it was a moment she had played in her head all the way from her dorm room until she stepped into the shower with him.

Surprisingly, Tom barely flinched or seemed surprised. She wondered whether his reaction was a testament to his cockiness or if he believed that she would come that made him so well prepared.

"Laura," he said in a tender yet masculine and sonorously pleasing voice. He couldn't back down now, but he was a gentleman, so he would act like one.

Something about the way he called her name felt different, and the thinned air she had felt earlier only grew thinner as her curiosity was piqued beyond reason. He remained at arm's length and said nothing else, but a flicker of a smile in the left-hand corner of his mouth appeared while his blue eyes shone beautifully against the bathroom lights.

Laura parted her lips and hoped to speak but found herself struggling to conjure words. She knew what she wanted to say to him, but for some reason, his stunning presence simply sucked away the words and made her insides swirl madly with butterflies. Laura remained silent while they traded unsaid words through curious stares until Tom made his first move.

Her heart stopped beating momentarily upon seeing his hand move closer to her shoulder, but he slowly veered it away and turned off the light switch just outside the shower, bringing them both into darkness. Laura gasped and tried not to look at the door for fear that she might make a run for it.

The lights! She thought to herself.

Being in the same bathroom with a man was terrible enough, and having the lights out sent her senses into a heightened state. The urge to leave grew. Hoping it would hide how nervous she was, her body froze as she held her breath.

"You came," he whispered and moved closer to her. She could feel his breath traveling the brief distance between them.

Laura tried to speak or at least utter a word to indicate she wasn't in any way mystified and too afraid to talk to him.

He drew near and whispered, "No words are necessary. Let's get you washed up."

Laura sighed in relief. He had no idea, but his decision to limit her from speaking helped her nerves gain some strength. Otherwise, she might have shuttered and bolted for the door. Tom slowly leaned his body into hers, and Laura closed her eyes and placed her hands over her breasts as she tried to shield herself as best as possible.

He made no move to take her last line of defense away as he rounded his arm over her waist and gently pulled her body closer to his. A soft gasp, filled with fear and a small amount of relief, escaped Laura's mouth. She could not entirely explain how she felt. He was gentle and took his time, which greatly confused her.

What is he doing?

Tom didn't make the moves she had expected of him or any typical man for that matter. Instead, he turned the shower head and slowly, with his hand still wrapped around her waist, guided her underneath it without ever letting go. Laura battled a bundle of worrisome thoughts in her head. She wondered why he wasn't speaking and what would come next. She had been there before with a man and the events had left her mentally and psychologically scarred. She was angry at herself for being so bold. *Why did I decide to do this? What was I thinking? I've completely lost my mind!*

Surprisingly to her, Tom's hand didn't seem to sting her skin where he held her. As he eased his grip from her waist, she felt the odd sensation of wanting him to hold her again. The thought left Laura baffled as she felt one of her hands slowly leave her breasts and search through the darkness for him. His soft hands left her trembling with so much ease that she slowly placed them back around her waist while she reached for his hair and dug her strong fingers through it gently.

Closing her eyes, Laura awaited the worst and told herself she could weather the storm regardless of whatever he might do to her. The euphoric sensation from the warm shower hitting her skin made her nerves tighten, and her teeth clench as she waited or at least expected the worst.

This will end badly. I will run screaming like a maniac, naked and wet, from this room. No Uncle Max! Stop Uncle Max! Please, Uncle Max! the words rang aloud in her head endlessly.

Suddenly, the voice disappeared. Tom drizzled some shampoo into his hands, and he began scrubbing her scalp gently while she felt the soothing relief from his touch massage her tenderly. His hands felt like they had come from heaven.

Releasing some pent of air in her chest, Laura gasped softly. Oddly, her heart wasn't racing anymore, and her body finally relaxed. He was gentle and soft. Taking care not to get soap in her eyes, Tom leaned her back gently to rinse the shampoo from her hair. He reached for a fresh washcloth just outside of the shower. He placed it under the stream of water, then worked it thoroughly with soap. He massaged her shoulders and set her stiffened nerves free as her spine grew in tingling sensation. Laura felt absolute relief. His touch was the best her skin had felt all her life, and it brought with it some strange sense of security that allowed her to permit him to glide his hands down her body without any restrictions.

Tom remained silent, but his hands spoke volumes in soothing tones as Laura felt her second hand finally drop from her breast and her shield, which had been sky high, totally crumbled to the ground as he washed her back clean and rinsed without making a move to seduce her. His purity cleansed her worried soul right there, and his sense of care cracked through her years-old walls.

Laura did not realize it, but life slowly felt meaningful. She wondered why he wasn't making any moves as his hands continued to move majestically back and forth, setting her skin alive and reigniting the dead parts she had carried with her for years.

"Woah," Laura whispered upon feeling his hand brush against her breast as he rinsed her thoroughly.

Tom chuckled a little and took a few seconds to reply, but he answered in an even softer tone, "I'm so sorry. I didn't mean to startle you, Laura?" "It's ummm…dark and a…"

She cut him off. "It's ok, Tom. You can keep washing."

You can keep washing?? *Ugg*, she thought to herself. *That was brilliant, Laura, really brilliant.* Typically, she was cold and hardened, full of sarcastic remarks when talking to most guys who tried to have anything to do with her. But with him, she could barely form a sentence.

She couldn't believe it. Feeling his hand on her breast had not caused her to feel sick, which was exactly what she had thought would happen. Unfortunately, feeling sick is what happened with every guy who ever touched them. She learned to muddle through the experiences, but they always left her feeling out of sorts and empty. Instead, with Tom and his gentle touches, her heart had begun pounding in the good way she only felt when excited about something. The butterflies in her belly swarmed around happily and prompted her to stretch her arms around his neck. Holding him firmly, she pulled him closer.

Tom made no move to resist but slowly shortened the gap between them as Laura felt her senses kick into focus and her body jolt with excitement. Nervous as hell as his warm breath broke through the chilly air and smeared its comfort on her face, she sucked in enough courage to continue as her heart felt tingly and her legs felt numb. She sought his lips through the darkness before finding them, readily parted, and waiting to receive hers. Laura felt her soul catch on fire and her spine grew with pleasure. Her body, rapidly electrified inch by inch. There were no words, but the moment felt perfect. His touch was tingly, and his lips were nothing short of awesome, for they merged perfectly with hers.

Laura wanted nothing more than to have a taste of those lips for the entire night through. Like butter melting away under the presence of his hotness, she felt her lips threaten to melt by the way he nibbled them and slowly began sliding his right hand from her waist up her side towards her neck. For the first time, without a care in the world, she slowly opened herself up and allowed his soft hands to pleasure her body as he continued to massage her shoulders and neck.

Leaning towards the ground and sneaking both hands underneath her buttocks, Tom paused and unlocked his lips from hers. He lifted her up and slowly carried her until he could pivot her against the bathroom wall. Masculine and tender, a mixture, Laura couldn't say she had encountered in a man throughout her whole life, Tom locked his lips back with hers and began working his kisses along her neck as Laura felt her breath escape heavily from her lips. Her heart felt like it could beat on forever without dying.

Like a rejuvenated engine, earthed in dirt and so much waste, Laura burst back into life as she grabbed his neck and dug her fingers into his back while his lips continued to melt away at her skin. His kisses moved across her collarbone, he neared her breast and he gently set her back down. His fingers sneaked their way into her hair as he pulled her head backward and opened her chest to the mercy of his lips.

Laura breathed in the air and exhaled but felt unable to complete any words. Although she felt so much pleasure with him, part of her still wanted to fight his touch every minute. She was incapable of allowing her body to let go entirely, and she didn't understand how to manage any of her thoughts and feelings in that moment.

Tom slathered more soap onto the cloth and began gently washing her arms. He tangled his fingers in between hers to wash them clean. With his hand in hers, they paused for a moment, and he stole another small kiss. Laura worked hard to continue to fight to allow herself to feel the pleasure.

Her body trembled, and her soul shuddered in ecstasy as her insides pleaded for more, but she could never say the words out loud. He had everything under control, and Laura gladly allowed him to continue taking charge.

Time trickled by without them knowing, and Laura, whose demons constantly ran wild within such confined spaces, wasn't sure she ever wanted to leave this space with him. Her demons were nowhere to be found, and she could barely recall images of her haunted moments in the shower with her Uncle Max while she was with Tom. Almost like a human shield blocking away her pain and torments, Tom's presence there with her was unquantifiable, and she wanted him with each passing second.

Laura closed her eyes briefly and drew in some more air while Tom kissed her body more and went down to her belly button, prompting her to lean against the corner of the shower. She feared her knees might buckle and cause her to topple over right there.

What are you doing to me? Something about the moment brought the realization that she wanted him. At least for now, or maybe forever. Tom gave her unspoken question no answer.

Licking her belly button briefly, he sent his lips south and stopped. He gently began to massage her legs and wash them clean. He worked his hands up and down, back and forth, side to side, wrapping his arms around her and gently massaging her buttocks. His warm lips slowly kissed her thighs as he cleansed them. Air became difficult to breathe, and she struggled for balance as he lifted her leg to caress and massage her foot. Bent down as low as he could manage, he moved his hands over the arch of her foot, pushing on the pressure points and then placing her foot down gently so he could switch to the other one.

"We can't let the other foot get jealous," he teased.

Like a masterful surgeon dissecting a major organ, his hands glided slowly along the outer edges of her body, and she felt herself wanting to surrender to him entirely. Laura felt her demons disappear, replaced by the angelic soul now caressing her body in heavenly pleasure.

She wanted him. She wanted everything he had to offer. She wanted the feeling of "life" he continued to breathe into her through his touch and actions. He had given thought to her, he cared for her, and he teased her with a shower to clean up from the day. That is exactly what he gave her and so much more.

Laura continued to fight the pleasure, but lesser now. Her eyes rolled desperately while her head moved from side to side as Tom worked his magic.

Laura looked at him, and while darkness mainly prevailed in the tight space they were cramped in, the beauty in his blue eyes she had explored before he turned off the bathroom lights continued to spur her on. Drawing him up for a kiss, she clasped her hand around his face. Their lips met once again in a tender, gentle fashion. She was scared, but not for reasons she expected. She was scared that she would fall completely in love with him, and he would be the one who would shatter the walls she worked so hard to build.

She nestled her head inside his chest like a perfectly fitted glove. He wrapped his arms around her and held her. She felt safe.

***

Morning bloomed in beauty and without the disturbing feelings Laura found herself typically accustomed to. Her skin felt perfect, and her soul felt sheltered, right there, tucked underneath Tom's arms, with affection beyond comparison.

Laura lay still, with her eyes closed as her thoughts wandered across her mind. She could hear him breathe and, even more, she could feel his warm hands underneath her head. The night was perfect. They slept tangled up in bed, and Laura wondered just before she slept what the morning might hold.

Slowly turning her head to the side and opening her eyes, she met with his, staring right back at her. His eyes, beautifully and brightly burning with compassion. Tom wore the kindest and most innocent smile. He gently ran his fingers through her hair as they remained in silence and continued to stare at each other.

"You believed I was going to come," Laura whispered.

Tom smiled and sighed aloud. "Honestly, I thought I didn't stand a chance in hell."

She chuckled and caressed his chest as he pulled her closer before turning her around so he could hold her from behind. Laura could feel his tempered storm poking right into her back, and it brought a warm smile to her cheeks. The handsome devil behind her was one of a kind. She didn't need a prophet to tell her that. The night before was evidence of just how much in sync everything about him was with her soul.

"Well, hello there," Laura purred as she felt his body press harder against hers.

Tom held her tighter and planted his lips into the back of her neck. "Good morning, beautiful."

TWENTY-FOUR

Fall 1996

T om asked in a soft but confused tone, "Did I do something?" He had managed to see almost all sides to Laura through their entire year of dating, but her current emotional state felt new. He wondered where it was coming from, and he sat up and reached for her shoulder so that he could turn her around. Laura resisted and brushed his hand away as she wept further and curled into a ball, shutting him out in the process.

She wished he had not seen her tears, and she knew he would think he caused them. Laura slowly pulled her comforter up over her body and looked at the other side of the bed to avoid Tom's gaze.

Sobbing and sniffing intermittently, "Please leave me alone," she pleaded.

Tom sat up on the side of the bed and wondered what he might have done wrong. With Laura, he could swear there was always something, from her endless outbursts and rage to her emotional switches, which often left him angry to no bounds. Yet there was something special about her he just could not ignore.

Hoping to elicit a response from her, "You and I need to talk about this," he demanded in a subtle tone. But Laura ignored him and continued to weep uncontrollably into her pillow without any word to her troubled boyfriend. Tom turned back to look at her, and reached for her shoulder once again, and pleaded, "Laura, will you please talk to me?"

Laura stiffened her shoulder and nudged his hand off before sitting up and staring blankly at him. Tom was scared but more worried that he had done something to hurt her. His heart felt heavy with worries, and his chest had begun to hurt, as the sight of Laura crying brought him nothing short of intense pain.

Tom called out to her once again, "Laura, please talk to me. Say something, anything at all."

Bobbing her head as though she had heard him, Laura sat up slowly and reached for his hand, "You've done nothing wrong. I promise," she said softly.

Tom couldn't believe her words even though she seemed to be telling him the truth. He could feel something was wrong with her, and she wasn't telling him for reasons he wished he could find out. Stubborn as ever when it came to her emotions, he turned away from her, stood up, and picked up his clothes.

Laura watched him begin to dress hurriedly but without showing any bit of anger or emotion. Tom got dressed in a minute, took another look at Laura, and with a loud and exhausted sigh, headed for the door. Laura watched Tom walk away, but he stopped by the door and said, "I swear to you that I love you, Laura. I love you more than you know, and I wish you'd let me in."

Laura wished she could speak but she held her words back as she watched Tom shed some tears before brushing them aside and walking out of the room.

Leaving her outstretched hand grasping nothing but air, "Tom!" she called out just a moment too late as he walked away. She wondered how she could begin to tell him what was bothering her.

Their relationship had just mended again after three months of distance between them. Laura had undoubtedly caused the break-up, but as always, Tom came back. His willingness to return to her wasn't a sign of weakness or that he was fickle with his emotions. He had promised that he would love her and be with her always.

Laura, however, couldn't help her demons from rearing their ugly head the way they did while he pinned her hands into the bed. The moment was reminiscent of what Uncle Max had done to her, and the scars felt real again, almost like they had just burst forth from the corners of her mind where she neatly had tucked them. His brutal touch and distasteful grip around her wrist on those nights and in that room had come rushing through like a flood of bitterness mixed with shame.

Laura, wondering if these episodes would continue to be part of her life forever, bowed her head and wept some more. Then, wiping away the tears from her eyes, she felt her heart yearn for Tom to come back into the room. Her entire world needed him, and everything within her wanted him dearly.

Dragging herself out from the bed and searching around the room for some clothes to put on, "Tom!" she yelled atop her voice. Laura was worried she might end up chasing the man she loved away because she wasn't sure how best to manage her emotions and pain. For tonight though, Laura hoped to try. Even if she couldn't break down her tall walls of steel that still sheltered her heart, she hoped to make peace with the one soul who loved her regardless of her shortcomings. The one soul, she knew could eventually break through her walls.

***

Laura dragged her feet along the sandy courts and searched around for the perfectly built man with soulful eyes, even if she wouldn't be able to see him in the darkness. She knew it was the one place he could be on such a night if he wanted to clear his head.

"Tom!" Laura called and searched some more.

With the bristling cold night air brushing her skin and her feet feeling sore as she dragged them through the sand, she felt nothing more than anger toward herself. She caused the pain Tom might be feeling. Her heart wasn't beating as fast as she had expected it would, but she was desperate to find him.

Regardless, she needed to find Tom and explain her feelings. She wasn't sure how much she could tell him, but her walls needed to come down a bit, even if opening up to him would be a tall order for her to carry out. She owed him that, at least. Her heart found strength for her to forge ahead, and her feet weren't planning on failing her. It seemed everything within Laura yearned for him to know the truth.

She paused to catch her breath before yelling one more time, "Tom!"

Feeling sad and tired, she strained her gaze ahead. A male figure slowly approached her, and her heart leaped in excitement as her insides tingled with joy. The figure resembled Tom as he neared, but disappointedly, it turned out to be someone else as he stared oddly and walked past her. Disappointed and dejected, Laura lowered her head and looked around for a place to sit.

"Hello!" the male voice called to her from behind.

Laura felt the butterflies flutter inside her stomach, as she tried hard not to react too quickly. The sound of his sweet voice always sent tingles through her body.

"What is a pretty girl like you doing out alone on a cold night at the volleyball courts?" He said slyly.

Laura smiled and wiped a tear from the corner of her right eye before finally turning around to look at him. She had so much she wished to say or could say, but the words felt heavy, and her heart wasn't strong enough to let them out. Tom never stopped staring at her with the loving gaze he had pinned on her from the first day they met.

His familiar and warm smile smoothed her heart with each passing second before laughing as she hurried towards him and into his arms. With her head placed against his chest and her arms tightened around his waist, she let out two words. "I'm sorry."

Tom slowly nodded his head and smiled. Leaning his chin on top of her head he said, "I know you are, babe. I know you are."

With Tom, life was simple. His love and affection for her discounted any wrongdoing or shortcomings, and she knew his feelings were genuine. She held him tightly and slowly reached for his buttocks, grabbing them firmly while she heard him laugh and slowly pull himself back from her.

"I'm truly sorry, and I swear to you that you've done nothing wrong," she said while looking into his twinkling blue eyes.

Tom smiled and placed a finger to her lips. "Babe, it doesn't matter. I want you to know I won't push you if you aren't ready to let me in on what's bothering you, but when you are ready, I'm here."

Laura paused and felt her eyes fill immediately with tears as she counted herself undeserving of him in every way.

"I love you," he whispered again. "I'm also sorry I took off like that. I simply needed some…"

Laura took her turn to stop his words by planting a kiss on his lips. He had done nothing wrong, and she wasn't going to have him drown himself in guilt for her issues that she didn't share.

"Tom, I'm ready to let you in." She took his hand and lead him to a spot at the picnic table, under the starry sky.

"When I was a little girl, I had an uncle who molested me. He did unspeakable things to me. It is difficult for me to talk about, I felt guilty for a long time. I was ashamed and embarrassed. It isn't something that you announce to people over lunch, you know." Tom's face looked so pained, and Laura could see her words were hurting him.

"I love you, and I feel safe with you, but I haven't been fair to you by keeping this secret. Sometimes, I have triggers that I'm not able to control and today was one of those moments. Although you didn't do anything wrong, my mind instantly took me back to a traumatic moment in my life. I am certain this is going to happen again, probably several times. I'll understand if my past is too much for you. You didn't sign up to deal with my emotional baggage. It's wrong for us to continue without you knowing and understanding."

Tom stood up and pulled Laura to him in the most comforting embrace he could provide. He silently hugged her for what felt like five minutes. "Laura, my heart is breaking for you. I want to kill him. Do I know this uncle?" Chuckling slightly at his remarks, she wiped her tears and relief filled her belly after letting her secret out. "You're an incredible woman, and you make me want to be a better man. I'll stick with you through thick and thin, this doesn't scare me away, but I need you to promise me that you'll talk to me about the moments when you're triggered. I don't want to do anything to hurt you or bring you pain. Ever!"

Laura nodded and validated his request by leaning in close and kissing him passionately.

Laura, accustomed to hiding her feelings, was complicated. She showed others only what she wanted them to see. Tom held the keys to unlock her secrets and bring her defenses down, he just didn't know he possessed the power. Tom had unlocked a small portion of her defenses that night and finally, Laura was glad to let him in.

"The stars look beautiful," Laura said with a smile. The two lay atop the picnic table talking and searching for constellations in the sky. Tom knew a great deal about the galaxy, and Laura loved to listen to him talk about it. The moon was full, and the sky was clear. As she lay with him, his warmth radiated through her entire body,

TWENTY-FIVE

Fall 1998

Laura could not believe it had been exactly two years since he first invited her into the shower, and each day felt like the millionth time they were falling in love with one another. Truthfully though, Laura had lost count in the number of times their relationship had hit the rocks and felt like it would end, but every time, they always seemed to find a way to pull it back together.

Laura smiled and stared at Tom's glistening eyes like they were the best pair of eyes she had ever come across in her life. She looked across the restaurant table at the man wearing the perfectly tailored suit and tie, a happy expression on his face and a smile lining his lips that forever melted her heart.

Tom cleared his throat and smiled at Laura. He took her hand from across the table into his and planted a kiss gently on the back of her hand. "You look stunningly beautiful tonight," he said.

She felt the flush of blood rush into her cheeks as Tom waved at the waitress.

"Why aren't we eating at our usual restaurant downtown?" Laura asked.

Tom shrugged and simply replied, "I thought we could shake things up, you know? Enjoy a nice meal in a new and refreshing spot."

A new restaurant sounded perfect, and Laura was glad she had decided to go for her low-cut, tightly fitted purple sundress. She sat at the table and watched the waitress approach and hand them each a menu. Tom smiled at the menu and picked some shrimp with lobster sauce, while Laura opted for chicken and pasta. She preferred eating a light entree and having two desserts. The first dessert was the cheesecake on the menu, and the second was the handsome man sitting directly across from her.

Their dinner was served, and Laura ate in silence while she eyed Tom like she wanted to grab hold of him from the other end of the table. He nervously ate his meal with subtle stares, mixed with loving smiles sent her way.

Twenty minutes passed, and he got to his feet. "I need to use the men's room."

Laura nodded and watched him disappear out of sight as she focused on her meal. The lights went out, and darkness engulfed the entire restaurant. Laura, somewhat relaxed and hoping the backup generator would kick in, sat upright and looked out the glass window. She counted a minute that turned to minutes and still no lights turned on in the restaurant.

Worried for Tom, who had still not returned, "Does anyone know what is going on?" she asked. She remained seated, unable to walk around in the darkness.

The room fell silent. Laura hated the dark and especially in a place that she wasn't familiar with. She reached for her purse hanging from the corner of her chair but found it missing.

"What on earth?" she muttered aloud.

Laura felt a rush of nerves run through her body and the silence crippled her emotions. She wondered what Tom was doing and if he had noticed the power was out.

"Excuse me!" Laura cried out loud.

It had been ten minutes or so now, and the lights still had not come back on. Frustrated and a little frightened at the same time, Laura slowly got up from her seat and watched the first light in the restaurant come on. Like a chain reaction, starting behind her at the farthest wall, the lights came back on systematically. She noticed the waiters and waitresses now standing in a row in the aisle that led to her table.

There was something odd about them. They all held white signs in their hands, as somewhat goofy smiles stretched across their faces. Laura ignored them for a moment and turned to look back at her table. Her heart leaped towards her mouth and her knees buckled out of her control, causing her to fall into her seat in an embarrassing heap as the blood drained from her face.

Laura opened her mouth to speak but fell short on words as she looked back at the wait staff, who had turned the white signs in their hands so she could see the gold letters printed on them. "SAY YES LAURA," they read.

Tom was down on one knee in front of their table. His smile was bigger than she had ever seen before, and in his hands was the most enormous and exquisite rock she had ever come across in her life.

He cleared his throat and drew closer, "Laura. My love."

Blushing as she listened to him speak romantically, Laura melted.

"Some men search a lifetime and never find the love they're looking for. Some find her but don't know it until it is too late. Only a few truly realize what they've found and thank the stars for true love. You are my one true love. Laura Christine Shirk, will you marry me?"

Laura nodded her head happily, "Yes! A thousand times yes!"

She held out her hand, and Tom slid the diamond ring onto her finger. The ring was a perfect fit. The diamond shone brightly in mesmerizing beauty.

"I love you," whispered Tom, remaining on his knee as Laura slowly stood from her seat.

She pulled him up with teary eyes and overwhelming excitement as she wrapped her arms around his neck and kissed him passionately. A loud hurray erupted from the restaurant staff and patrons sitting nearby. The manager brought over a large chocolate cake; the icing swirled to form a heart on top. Confetti and small flowers decorated the plate, Tom had ordered their best dessert to commemorate the moment.

Staring at the cake, Laura said in a shocked tone, "You planned all this without telling me?" Looking around she noticed the staff was gleaming and smiling at her and Tom.

"Congratulations!" they chorused.

Laura laid her head onto Tom's chest and broke into tears. She wondered how someone as emotionally and psychologically broken as she could land a man who truly loved her, who was willing to fight for her, and who genuinely cared about her happiness.

With her head still resting on his chest, he whispered, "I know our relationship isn't always perfect, I'm not perfect. But I promise to be the best man I can be for you." Laura did not doubt anything he said. Her only doubts were of herself.

TWENTY-SIX

Summer 1998

T om had barely parked the car and turned off the ignition when his bride-to-be jumped out of the car, raced through the parking garage, and headed for the front door.

"Something is wrong with her. I can feel it. I could hear it in her voice!" Laura mumbled in a troubling tone as she barged through the hospital's main entrance and almost knocked a woman over. Peeping into the wards on her right, she continued to veer ahead, she hoped to catch sight of the woman without going through much fuss. Unfortunately, Samantha wasn't there, and it only enraged Laura more.

"Excuse me!" she quivered at the lady at the front desk.

"Good afternoon, ma'am. How may I help you?" the bespectacled young lady with a thin smile replied.

"My mother, Samantha Shirk was brought in here not long ago. Can you tell me what floor she is on?"

The young lady looked down the hallway leading away from the burn unit. "Head down the hallway, take the elevator to the third floor and ask to see Dr. Pat."

Tom had just walked into the hospital when he saw Laura, barely caring about anyone around her as she hurried over to the elevator. Waving at the lady behind the front desk, Tom raced after his soon-to-be wife. He halted upon noticing the look on the nurse's face when she asked him not to run on the hospital floors.

"Laura! Laura, wait for God's sake!" he called to her and reached for her shirt to try and catch up with her.

She brushed his hand off and began punching the elevator button impatiently, but it would not come open. "Open, damn it!" she said.

Finally catching up with her, Tom stepped between Laura and the elevator doors. His hands were gently raised, indicating he meant no harm. "Laura! Laura, listen to me!"

Laura, impatient as ever, tried to maneuver her way around Tom. "Something is wrong, Tom! You didn't hear her on the phone. I did, and I tell you, she didn't sound well!"

Tom shook his head and sighed, "We can't run along these floors, babe. This is a hospital. You don't know anything yet, so let's try and remain calm, okay?"

Breathing deeply, Laura nodded her head as Tom tried the elevator button again. The relief in her eyes when she saw the doors chime open was immeasurable, prompting her to leap right in as Tom followed behind her. He watched her punch on the number three button nervously. Trying unsuccessfully to contain her thoughts, she began to pace within the tightly squared cubicle.

Tom drew her closer, wrapped his arms around her waist, and whispered into her ear, "Everything will be all right."

"What if something is terribly wrong?" she asked in a paranoid tone. "I don't think I have the strength for this. I doubt I have…"

Cutting her off, Tom locked her in a rather deep gaze and said, "You can handle whatever news you receive today. You're the strongest person that I know, and I'll be with you every step of the way."

The words came out in a simple stretch, but they automatically calmed her nerves. Tom always knew what to say, and while Laura sensed something wasn't quite right with her mother, she found strength and reassurance from his words.

The elevator finally stopped moving, and the doors slowly opened. Laura saw three doctors in their scrubs walking down the corridor. She chased after them when one mentioned Samantha's name.

"Is that my mother you're talking about? The nurse downstairs told me to meet with Dr. Pat about my mother, Samantha Shirk, who was rushed here a few hours ago."

The three doctors shared a rather glum look before the oldest of the three stepped forward with an outstretched hand, "My name is Dr. Patrick Denver, and I am the oncologist assigned to your mother's case."

Laura's heart sank immediately, and had Tom not walked over to hold her hand, she might have fallen to the floor.

"You deal with cancer patients, don't you?" Laura asked in a strained tone.

Taking note of his elegance and obvious maturity, she eyed the doctor from head to toe as he explained what he understood to be wrong with Samantha. The words simply flew past her ears as she drowned her consciousness in the nice shoes he wore. It was the only strategy she could use to block out the words he was saying.

"If you want to see her, you can go to her room, but she must remain in the hospital for further treatment," he said and finally ended his lengthy prognosis.

Laura felt numb in every nerve in her body as Tom asked for directions to Samantha's room.

***

Hospitals were one of the places that made Laura's skin crawl. Staring through the doorway at her sick mother sleeping with her dad by her side, she wondered what her mom must be going through and how painful the entire experience must be for her. It had been three months in and out of the hospital, and the chemo was beginning to take its toll. Her father was exhausted, not leaving Samantha except for a few hours here or there to clean up and get a fresh change of clothes.

"I hate seeing her like this," Laura whispered to Tom as they walked into the room. She had aged what seemed a full twenty years in three months and was barely recognizable as the beautiful, spunky woman she once was.

Tom smiled and said, "Your mother is a strong woman, and I'm sure she's going to pull through this."

His voice was shaky, and it showed that even he wasn't sure what to expect. The doctors had said cancer had spread to her lymph nodes, meaning it was moving erratically, and there was the possibility it was more life-threatening than they initially thought.

Laura whispered, "Mom. Moommm." Lying in bed, Samantha slowly turned and smiled at her.

"I thought you two would keep on bickering and staring at me like I am some kind of postcard while you stood at the door all day long," Samantha joked. "Hello, kids."

Tom waved his hand respectfully and replied, "Hello Mrs. Samantha. How are you feeling today?"

Entering the room, Laura sat by her mother's bed as Tom pulled a chair closer and stared at the machines directly linked to Samantha's body. The sight was troubling, so he looked away to focus his gaze on Laura.

"Well, I've seen better days." Samantha coughed and struggled to breathe as Laura helped her rest her head on the pillow more comfortably. "I wasn't expecting you two today. What's the surprise?"

Tom smiled and shrugged, but he stared at Laura, hoping she would tell her mother their reason for showing up unannounced. Laura began to speak but then urged Tom to do the talking.

"Is there something going on between you two that I should know?" Samantha asked her daughter before looking at Tom.

Tom got to his feet and cleared his throat, "We were thinking about moving the wedding up a couple of months, so that you might be feeling better, Laura wants nothing more than for you to be there."

Laura nodded and toyed with the ring on her finger. Taking her daughter's hand into hers, Samantha smiled and remained silent.

"I still cannot believe it. My baby, my daughter is getting married," Samantha said.

Laura could not believe it either, but she was glad beyond words that the wedding was indeed going to happen. Looking out the window so they could no longer see her face, Samantha lifted Laura's hand closer to her lips and kissed it tenderly.

"Mom," Laura said to her. "What's wrong?"

Samantha gently rubbed her face with her hand and looked back at her daughter, "It hurts," she simply said.

The words hurt Laura even more than the cancer ravaging her mother's body. Seeing the usually strong and vibrant woman bedridden and having to live her life dependent on machines made Laura sick to her stomach.

"It hurts badly, darling, and..." she paused a moment, "and I don't know if I can take any more," Samantha said.

Her eyes filled with water, and her lips trembled as Laura caught onto the "sad train," and they soon both began wiping each other's faces clean of their tears. Tom, feeling sorry for Samantha, but not pity because she wouldn't want that from him, remained in his seat. Her pride remained intact as always, even in her lowest time, and he could not respect anyone more than he did Samantha at that moment.

Laura assured her mother with her hands trembling, "You're going to get better. You're going to get better because Dad needs you, and so do I. We all do."

The words brought only a faint smile to Samantha's face, for she knew something her daughter and the rest of her family didn't know.

"I want you to be strong for me, Laura." Samantha said, "I need you to be, regardless of what happens and no matter how things might turn out."

Laura sat back and frowned at her mother. "You need to focus on getting better and not saying things like that."

Tom finally found an avenue to speak, "Yes, Mrs. Samantha, you should focus on getting better so we can continue to play golf at your favorite course and I can pick those yellow lilies you love so much."

Samantha's eyes widened, and a broader smile grew on her weary face. "Yes! Those lilies you brought me were beautiful. And you know I always love whooping your butt in golf too," she said chuckling. She knew full well she had never beaten him on the golf course. Speaking in a more serious tone, she said "I need you to promise me you'll take care of her, Tom. She's my baby and one special girl."

Tom nodded his head and smiled. "I promise you that I'll do just that."

Samantha looked frail but very happy as she waved Tom over and held his hand tightly in her fragile, cold, and shaky hands. Tom felt his smile lessen as he looked at Laura, who was in denial about how far her mother's illness had progressed. He wondered if Samantha would tell her or if the doctors had something new to share about her cancer.

Samantha managed a smile, the one thing she was perfect at, even in the face of peril. Tom seemed to understand the smile. She wanted his trust and promise not to hurt her daughter. She wanted him to give his word that he would treat Laura fairly, regardless of her shattered heart, she wanted confirmation that he would love and respect her always.

TWENTY-SEVEN

Three Weeks Later

Tom and Laura had almost completed the eight-hour drive down the Interstate once again. The plan was to head straight to the hospital. Laura, leaning back in her seat, stared at the man who was going to become her husband in less than three months.

He is hiding something from me.

Tom wasn't one to hide things from her, but she could tell just by looking at him. He could barely make eye contact with her.

"Tom."

Tom nodded and fixed his gaze on the road before responding, "Yes, Sweetie?"

Laura waited for a few more seconds, but Tom said nothing other than those two words.

"You've barely said anything to me through the entire trip. Are you keeping something from me?" Laura asked.

Tom shrugged and replied, "Err... nothing. Nothing is wrong, I'm not keeping anything from you."

Laura took his word for the truth, but his lack of answers left her suspicions running. She wondered if the wedding plans were taking a toll on him, which he obviously would not share with her. He'd rather keep up his usual calm demeanor.

Laura said, "I can't wait to show mom the wedding dress I picked out." She looked out the car window and smiled. "I'm sure she'll love it," Tom replied.

Pulling the car to a halt, Tom remained silent as Laura wondered what they were doing on the side of a busy road. He looked at her with his eyes red and his lips moving subtly, but never uttering any words. Laura was worried now, imagining a million things that could be upsetting him.

She could see through his façade. Something was definitely bothering him, and she was slowly chipping away at him, like a sandcastle smoothed over by endless tides.

"Tom, what's going on?" Laura asked as she placed her hand on his shoulder. "Are you getting cold feet about our wedding?"

Tom wished he could tell her the truth, but there was no telling how she would respond. His heart yearned to spill everything he thought. He knew Laura had convinced herself that Samantha would be okay, and he didn't want to break her heart.

Wearing an innocent smirk, Laura reached for his face and wiped the tears rolling down his cheeks with her thumb. "If this is about you getting cold feet, we can talk about it. I'm scared too, but I know that I love you, and I know that you love me," she said tenderly.

Tom nodded his head gently and sighed. "Yes... I... I don't know...."

Laura laughed and leaned over to plant a kiss on his lips. Staring at him acting like a baby made her heart jolly. His expression helped her heart understand that Tom, regardless of his size and muscle mass, was nothing but a baby yearning for love on the inside. He was her baby through and through, and she could not love him more.

"Let's go see my mom, and maybe we'll still have time to stop at the wedding venue before they close, ya big cry baby," she teased.

Stealing glances at Laura every chance he got, Tom began to drive again. He wondered when they arrived at the hospital and the moment of truth revealed itself, what would happen to the smile Laura presently wore across her face. The world felt brutal and wicked. He knew Samantha didn't have much time left. Laura would deny it, but he would be there to help her through it.

As Tom's hands tightened around the steering wheel and his foot floored the gas, he felt the impending sadness grow within his gut. Staring at him blankly, Laura wondered what had come over him.

***

Arriving at the hospital earlier than expected seemed to make Laura happy. This would give them more time for the wedding arrangements when they were finished visiting her mother. Planning a wedding from eight hours away wasn't an easy task, every time Laura came home to visit, she scheduled time to plan the wedding.

Looking somber, Tom stepped out of the car. Laura, continuing to chalk his behaviors up to his lack of desire for more wedding planning, didn't take him seriously. Laura exited the car and the two walked a few car lengths toward the hospital until Laura paused.

"Isn't this Mary's car?" she asked in a perplexed tone before noticing another familiar plate parked just a few feet from her sister's. "This is Matthew's car too."

Tom felt his heart break for Laura as they continued to walk toward the entrance. Laura wondered why her siblings had gone to the hospital without telling her. It wasn't like Mary and Matthew to exclude her.

She turned to Tom immediately. "Did you know my brother and sister would be here?"

Tom shook his head, "No."

Laura's heart was racing and her instincts were on fire, as she pushed open the hospital doors. She felt her stomach suddenly grow dead with each passing second as she neared the hallway to Samantha's room. As she turned the corner, Laura caught sight of her siblings.

Looking distraught, Matthew and Mary sat on a bench with their hands in between their legs just outside their mother's room. Laura caught their attention, and she managed a wave.

Tom stepped aside and leaned his back against the wall as Laura walked past him toward her brother.

"Matthew?" she asked her brother as she looked through a small slit in the door to her mother's room. Laura could see several nurses inside fiddling with some of the machines. Dr. Pat stood and smiled weakly at Samantha who didn't seem to acknowledge his presence there at all. Feeling something wasn't right, Laura started to go into the room but she felt Matthew's hand hold her back.

293

"Laura don't!" he yelled.

"Let go of me, Matthew!"

Tom walked over, as did Mary. The three formed a ring around Laura to keep her contained as the medical team did their work inside the room. Laura didn't live near home anymore, and she was always the last to know what was going on with her family. Dr. Pat, with a somber expression on his face, noticed the ruckus brewing outside and waved at the nurses as he stepped out of the room.

"What's going on, Doctor?" Laura asked while the trio continued to guide her back.

The doctor waved at them and asked that she be let free. "We have prepared her, and she has been asking to see you."

Confused and unsure of what to make of his words, Laura felt unable to move and cross over the threshold between the corridor and her mother's room. The nurses exited as Dr. Pat also turned around to leave, allowing Laura's mind to interpret everything she had just witnessed.

"Laura," Mary whispered to her little sister. "Mom wants to see you."

Laura nodded and slowly turned to look at the frail figure on the bed. Stepping inside the room, she felt like a void had enveloped her completely. The room was deathly quiet and lacked happiness.

Sounding as though she was fearful of breaking the women with her voice, Laura whispered, "Mom," in the most hushed tone she could summon.

Laura took her mother's frail hand into hers. She thought she heard something snap as she held onto it gently. The months had not been kind, but Laura had held onto just about enough hope every time she walked through the door to visit her ailing mom.

"Laura," her mother whispered back, barely managing to complete her name.

Hearing her own heart begin to drum wildly inside her ribcage, Laura leaned closer to Samantha who was struggling to turn her head and look into Laura's eyes. The EKG monitor recorded close to a flat line on its readings, which caused Laura to realize the worst was near.

"I'm sorry," the weakened woman whispered. "I'm so so sorry, Laura."

Laura shook her head and managed not to let the tears swelling in her eyes drop. "You have nothing to apologize for. Everyone's here to see you, Matthew and Mary are outside your room, and of course, Dad hasn't left your side once this entire time."

Laura felt the weakened grip loosening around her hand, and with each passing second her mother's breath became even harder to come by. Samantha was laboring hard to remain alive, and Laura wondered how she had not noticed the signs a few weeks before when she came to visit. She had chosen not to see it.

"Please, momma, please don't do this!" Laura begged.

She didn't need the doctor coming in to tell her what a "final meeting" for closure felt like. She was present in one, and apparently, everyone knew about it except her. Tom's silence during their trip began to make sense as did her siblings' unexpected presence.

"It hurts Laura," Samantha whispered. "It hurts bad."

The woman, previously a symbol of strength and unwavering guile, had been reduced to a weak and teary person lying in a bed and barely able to hold onto her daughter's hand.

"My wedding is in a few months, Momma," Laura reminded her with watery eyes, hoping it would give her the strength to stay alive. "You promised to see me walk down the aisle and marry the man of my dreams."

Laura's lungs collapsed, and she gasped for air. Feeling a panic attack approaching, she struggled to hold onto Samantha's hand. She managed the weakest smile that slowly began to fade from her face with each passing second.

"Be strong, Laura; we raised you to be strong. You... will... make... a... wonderful... bride... and..." Samantha paused and caught her breath. "... a wonderful mother, I love you, and don't forget three very important things. Always remember that when life hands you lemons, make lemonade. Always keep your eyebrows waxed. Always wear clean underwear and keep your legs shaved; you never know when you might be in a car accident and need medical attention."

Of course, these are the things my mother would say to me while she is on her death bed. She was always frantic about looking put together. I can't believe this is happening. It really can't be happening.

Laura shook her head aggressively and began to cry at the top of her lungs.

"Nooooooooooooo!"

Tom came rushing into the room as Samantha's hand left Laura's. The EKG machine read a complete flat line. Samantha had passed.

"Babe!" Tom cried out to Laura, but she could barely hear his voice over the sound of the EKG monitor telling her in the only way it knew how that her mother had just died. The strong-willed woman had succumbed to the devastating and unfair clutches of cancer. Laura wasn't sure how to process that Samantha was gone and kept grasping for her mother's hand.

Placing tender kisses all over her face, Paul hugged Samantha and held her tightly. Finally, Laura stopped struggling, while Tom wrapped his arms around her to give her support and comfort in an obvious time of need. Her world felt shattered into a zillion pieces for the umpteenth time, and the earth seemed to stop rotating just within that fraction of a second before her mother passed away.

"Laura," Mary reached over to console her little sister, but Laura was far from being mentally accessible to any of them at that moment. Instead, her long-standing walls began to re-erect themselves around her heart once again.

Hoping to evade the reality that had just struck her like a live wire, her mind desperately desired a haven to hide away. Events passed in slow motion, causing her to breeze past everything like a hollow shadow with no emotions as she fought hard to comprehend what turn of events had just taken place in her life.

"Talk to me, Laura!" Tom begged, trying to shake her back into consciousness.

Trapped in a world of pain and mental sadness that became the only place her mind seemed capable of understanding, Laura remained still. The feeling was worse than when her Aunt Penny died. Her emotions weren't quantifiable. She wished she could rationalize the moment, so her mind could find some escape or solace.

Silent and without tears rolling out of her eyes anymore, Laura ignored everything in the room and stared blankly at her mother, looking at what used to be a vibrant soul within a healthy body. What remained on the bed wasn't what she could relate to: the weakened, empty shell devoid of the beautiful person that nurtured her into existence and stood by her even through the most trying of times. Her mother was one of two people that knew about the devil and his misdeeds, and now she was gone. Dying with her was a substantial piece of Laura's strength and courage.

Trying to break through to her, "Laura!" Tom yelled again.

For Laura, the world suddenly lost its warmth and dragged along in nothing but a cold abyss with sinking soil. Everything worthy of the world, or her world, seemed to have left with the last breath escaping her mother's body. She felt the world had dealt her another terrible blow, and it had done it just a few months before the promise of perfection when she was to wed the love of her life.

"Tom," Laura whispered.

Tom stood before her, his eyes swollen with tears and his hands trembling, for he couldn't hold back how sad he felt as well.

"My mom needs to wake up," Laura whispered.

Tom held her tightly to his chest, and she made no move to fight. It was obvious she wasn't accepting the reality before her.

Twenty-Eight

Eighteen Months Later

T om sat at the edge of the bed, his head bowed, eyes closed, and a migraine slowly setting in as his wife continued to scream at the top of her lungs. Her voice, bouncing back and forth, echoed through the house and brought him to the edge of sanity. He wanted her to stop, or at least refrain from shouting. Laura was still struggling from her mother's death, which caused her to be extra emotional.

"Babe, please," he pleaded several times, but he felt too weak to lift his head this time.

Laura paused and stared at him, grabbed hold of the lamp on the night table, and swung it hard in his direction, prompting Tom to duck. The lamp missed, but grazed the left side of his face and clattered into the wall behind him. He looked over to his wife and felt his head threaten to implode with so much pent-up anger.

"Talk to me, Tom!' Laura yelled to his face. "Talk to me and stop acting like you're deaf or something!"

Tom got to his feet, looked around the room for his car keys, realized they were in the living room, and headed for the door. Laura moved faster than he had expected and stood in between him and the door. Daring him in every way possible, she pushed his silence to the point most men would have broken.

Sighing in frustration, he shouted angrily, "What do you want, Laura? I don't know what you want. I love you, but…"

Running his hand through his hair in frustration, he turned back around, and wondered where things had gone wrong this time around. Only two days had passed since their biggest fight yet. He could not understand the sudden switch and how Laura could change from a sensitive, loving, and caring woman to the one filled with rage and anger standing before him.

"Why are you doing this?" he asked. "Why are you trying to make things so hard? It's been eighteen months! Eighteen long months and we've had no peace or quiet in this house!" Tom knew how to push her buttons and send her over the edge. Sometimes, he felt the only way to get her to express what was going on in her head was to push her to her boiling point.

Laura cried softly as she leaned on the wall behind her for some support. She could see the frustration in his eyes and the tiredness from the endless fights.

"Please," Tom begged. "Just leave the conversation be for tonight."

Tom dropped his head and walked past her. Moving as fast as his legs would carry him, he hoped to make it to the front door before her and away from the toxicity for the night. He made it to the living room, alone and thankful, but with his headache fully taking root.

The pictures on the walls reminded him of the beautiful day she promised to be his wife forever. They were both smiling. Over time, he learned that Laura's true smile was in her eyes. He knew she struggled with darkness from her past. A burden they continually worked on together when she would let him inside her ten-inch-thick walls. He missed seeing the smile in her eyes, since Samantha passed.

Watching Tom stare at the framed pictures on the wall of their wedding, Laura crept to the living room and smirked. "I didn't want to marry you anyway, but you insisted. You insisted that I was feeling hurt from the loss of my mom."

Her words didn't make an atom of sense. They had picked the date long before Samantha passed, and they had her and Paul's blessing to marry.

"You don't make any bit of sense!" he yelled at her in response for the first time. "You keep getting angry and acting like a crazy person. I don't even know how to talk to you anymore. Everything you do just annoys the shit out of me. How we even ended up together is beyond me!"

Laura cackled wickedly and paused oddly for a brief second. "You think I'm a crazy person, Tom? You don't understand why we are together?"

Tom understood the situation was about to get worse. He had struck a nerve by pushing too far, and his options were either to run like hell or fake a heart attack. Faking a heart attack wouldn't save him from her, so he decided to run like hell. Watching his wife storm off and head back into their bedroom, Tom jumped towards the door and began fumbling with the lock to get it open.

"I'll show you crazy!" she yelled while she returned with a golf club in hand.

Shoving the door open, Tom raced out into the yard, and watched his wife follow him angrily without relenting.

"You don't think we should be together?" she yelled at him. "You have no idea what I've been through! You have no idea how I feel. Just go, just freaking go and never come back!"

"You're right. I don't know because you don't tell me. Laura, you won't talk to me!"

Golf club in hand, she charged towards him. He grabbed her as she lunged and pulled her into a tight hug, squeezing her arms by her side so that she couldn't use them. He held her tightly until she stopped squirming.

Damn him and his warmth, she thought.

The calming effect took several minutes, but his firm hug eventually squeezed all the anger right from her body, like the most wonderful security blanket ever made.

"Tom," Laura whispered "I'm sorry. I haven't been myself. I know I'm shutting you out, I don't mean to do it, but I've been through too much. I don't know how to share my burdens, even with you. I'm sad, Aunt Penny is gone, my mom is gone, and Uncle Max still creeps into my dreams at night. I'm afraid I'll never be good enough for you or our family."

Laura couldn't quite shake her demons, she feared they would haunt her forever. *How could she be a wife, a mother, and even a grandmother one day?*

Tom replied in an even more loving tone, "Babe, you are more than enough. I wish you could see yourself through my eyes."

Suddenly, Laura looked down at her legs. She began sobbing and slowly held up her blood-covered hand for Tom to see.

"Oh God!" he bellowed in a hurting tone. "Laura! What is happening?"

"We need to go to the hospital!" she shouted.

Racing to the car, his hands trembled as he struggled to put the key in the lock on the car door. His pregnant wife was in danger, and he felt helpless.

***

Laura opened her eyes to the sight of the white-colored room and the smell of ammonia so pungent in the air it almost made her want to puke. Her heart began to race. She barely moved. She hoped it was all a bad dream that would unfold into the reality of waking up inside their bedroom. Some part of her told her otherwise, and it would mean battling the endless thoughts of the last time she had been in the hospital.

Her hands began to tremble as she remembered the icy cold feeling of her mother's touch just before she took her last breath. Her legs tensed as she struggled to contain the streams of anxiety, slowly nearing a panic attack and coursing through her entire body. Laura hoped she might receive some good news; she closed her eyes again and whispered a few prayers.

Regardless of her hopes and prayers, upon opening her eyelids, the bright light rushed in, bringing with it the clear vision of a hospital ward with trays and an ultrasound machine just to her right, and no Tom.

I need to get out of here! I can't be here! She battled with herself and struggled to breathe.

"Tom!"

Gaining some clarity, she remembered the worried face of her sweet husband. He was driving like a mad man racing to the hospital and assuring her that everything was going to be okay.

Slowly sitting up, she wondered where Tom had gone. Thoughts of whether he had made a run for it and chosen never to return crossed her mind. She knew that Tom had promised to stick with her through thick and thin, but admittedly she had been a little much to deal with lately. There was no denying their marriage hadn't been sunshine and roses for quite some time. Her heart yearned for him, and her eyes swept around the room in hopes he was seated somewhere taking a nap.

Hoping he would come to her rescue and whisk her away from the hospital, "Tom!" she cried aloud for her knight in shining armor.

Pushing the door open and walking in with his usual smile as if he had telepathically heard her speak, Tom pulled up a chair, found a spot by her bed, and sat down without saying a word as he reached for his wife's hand and took it in his.

Laura stared at him and felt her lips move as she said weakly, "I'm sorry."

Tom shook his head and declined her apology. "No. I'm sorry, Laura."

Reaching for his head with her hand, Laura slipped her fingers into his hair and stared at him perplexed. She toyed with him as her husband dropped his head onto her belly and sobbed softly.

"Tom," Laura attempted to raise his head slowly.

Shrugging hard against moving, he got to his feet and began to pace around the room while Laura sat and watched the man unravel.

Tom turned and looked at his wife with sadness in his eyes. "Laura. We lost the baby."

Laura's world felt like it had come to an end yet again as she watched Tom's face. She could tell his pain grew with each passing second, and she blamed herself for it all.

"We will be fine," she mumbled in a show of strength for her embattled and troubled husband. "We'll be fine, honey."

Locking him in a long gaze, Laura raised her husband's head, leaned over, and planted her lips onto his. Losing the baby was hard for her, but Tom looked more distraught than she had ever seen him. Laura had decided she would be strong this time around for her husband and her family.

"My heart is breaking for you, Laura, but we'll get through this and everything else that comes our way," Tom said gently.

***

Not again!

It was spring 2003, Tom had barely stopped to catch his breath, his sweat-drenched shirt clung tightly to his body and his legs moved faster than his brain would allow him to think. He shoved aside anyone in his way so he could find out what exactly had happened to Laura.

The onlookers' eyes trailed him as he raced down the hall towards the same room she was in the other two times they rushed her to the hospital.

His eyes starting to water, *this cannot be happening again*, Tom thought to himself.

By comparison, the first one was the least traumatic; Laura had fought hard to remain sane. But the second miscarriage had been nothing but a trip to hell since it happened about six months back. With it came endless moping, countless contemplation of self-loathing, and outbursts of emotions whenever she saw other parents passing by with their kids.

"Why don't we deserve a child like they do?" she had asked Tom on one occasion while they were boarding a flight. "Are we not worthy? What have we done wrong to piss off the universe?"

Tom knew that Laura had been through so much, his heart ached for his Angel babies, but it hurt even more for his beautiful wife. She didn't deserve what life had dealt her. The self-blame only got worse, and the sleepless nights with fights became a norm around the house. It was why he prayed hard for good news after the hospital staff called him to tell him his wife had been rushed into the ER.

"You need to come quickly," the voice on the other end of the phone said.

Please be good news, he recited before halting at the end of the hall.

Laura was bound to be in one of the three rooms to his right. Wondering how he would console her if things went south, Tom desperately wanted to find his wife and hoped that news would be positive. Stepping out of the room, the doctor saw Tom and waved him over, they were practically on a first-name basis at this point.

"How's Laura, where is she?" Tom asked.

The young gynecologist nodded towards the room before patting Tom on the back and whispering, "She needs you now more than ever. Be strong."

The doctor's words sealed the deal. His wife had just had her third miscarriage, and nothing looked like a light at the end of her tunnel. Tom loved Laura more than words could express, but he feared his wife had about all she could handle. He didn't know how she could overcome this tragedy and push forward with her life, but he knew no matter what that he would be there with her.

Twenty-Nine

Fall 2003

With his eyes staring directly into hers, Tom sighed and held Laura's hands. He said to her gently, "I don't care if we have children. Yes, I'd love to have them, but if we can't have them, I will always love you and no other woman till the day I die."

Laura wanted to believe his words, but she knew too well the world they lived in wasn't perfect. The thought that they may not be able to have children, had eaten at her for the past few years and had begun to define each action she took with Tom.

"I just wish you'd tell me what exactly is going on in your head," Tom implored. "Every time I ask you, it's the same answer. And now, out of the blue, you want to go home by yourself for a week."

Laura wished she could tell him what her journey was about, but the truth was, even she wasn't sure what it would bring her. But ever since the letter landed in her mailbox and she read it, the handwritten words on the dull white paper were all her mind could think about.

Packing her bags, she said, "You'll have to trust me, Tom," without considering a word from him about her leaving.

His eyes showed his reservations, wondering if the woman was about to leave him. She was shutting him out again, but this time was different. Laura wasn't talking at all, and her behavior scared him to death.

He turned and asked again, "Can I at least come with you?"

Laura shook her head and paused for a minute to gather her thoughts. *This is something I need to do by myself, I need to find closure.*

Laura felt for him. She loved him dearly, but she couldn't give him a child of his own, and the insecurity tore her up inside. The years had trickled away with her being on the brink of depression, and his love kept her moving forward, even if she felt she didn't deserve it. He was medicine for her soul, and she couldn't give him the one thing he desired, a child. Laura used to tell herself that Samantha was in heaven looking after their Angel babies and eventually she would help them have children on earth. Regardless, it weighed heavy on

Laura, she assumed in her heart that it wasn't meant to be.

Tom finally conceded, "I don't understand, but I'll support you. I trust that whatever you're doing is for a good reason. I just want you to be happy."

Laura, wishing she could tell Tom everything about her dreadful past experiences with Uncle Max, stayed silent because telling him would mean haunting him with her demons. She had always done her very best to give him the cliff notes version because she wanted to protect him. Just as he continually protected her with his love, charm, and affection. Tom knew enough to understand, but she wasn't ready to share the entire truth. She was afraid it would torment him so much that he wouldn't be able to love her anymore.

Leaning over to kiss him, she said, "I'll be back in a few days, I promise," as she ran her finger along his handsome face, grateful for his unwavering love.

Laura knew that he deserved all of her, but there were pieces that she kept locked up tightly. The secrets she concealed inside of Pandora's box that she had refused to open. As much as Tom loved her and stood by her, she wasn't ready to allow herself to be completely vulnerable, even with him. She had survived the years by keeping everyone out, but she knew that Tom deserved to be fully let in.

Heading for the door, Laura walked outside and got into the cab waiting at the end of the driveway. She felt certain this was what she needed to do. For the first time in years, she felt positive about herself. However, the thought of following through with her plan also brought a substantial number of butterflies or rather moths to her stomach.

Are you sure you want to do this? She asked herself, sitting there and staring blankly at the cab driver who awaited instructions from her.

Living through times of absolute victimization, she often felt dead inside, but getting the fateful news two days back brought her renewed hope towards finally unshackling herself and finding some sanity.

Breathing deep, Laura said, "Take me to the airport."

The car zoomed off as Tom was standing in the doorway watching his wife leave. She could tell he wanted to chase the cab down and plead to her with everything he had. He could do it and had done it many times in the past. Especially, when she threatened to leave. Laura told him she felt it wasn't fair to stay because she couldn't bear his children.

"You are my world," he would say, his beautiful blue eyes looking into hers. "You are my soulmate, I will always be by your side, child or no child."

His sweet words resonated through her mind as she sobbed softly, not noticing the cab driver was staring at her through his rearview mirror.

I love you, and this is why I have to do this, she whispered through her heart and wiped her tears away as the car vanished into the night.

***

Staring at her watch and walking briskly down the corridor, Susie turned around as Laura followed behind her. Raising her brow, Susie said, "I don't know why you came, but thanks anyway. Almost everyone I told of the news barely reached out to me."

Laura wondered if there was a reason why no one else contacted Susie. She felt the urge to simply reply by saying maybe it was because the man was heinous and despicable, but she did well to keep her opinion to herself.

Arriving at the front desk, "Miss Susie!" a dark-haired nurse with a crooked grin called out to them.

"Hello, Pam," Susie waved back as they both neared the nurse. "I came to see my father. I was told he had been transferred to this floor, but Dr. Ross isn't in his office, so can you help me?"

Nurse Pam stared at Laura oddly and looked back at Susie.

"Oh, this is my cousin, Laura."

"It's nice to see another member of the family besides you," Pam teased as the three ladies laughed. "Follow me."

Pam and Susie were talking, but Laura wasn't paying attention. She couldn't help but smile to herself the farther they walked along the corridor. The note Susie had sent remained in her coat pocket, and the words crudely scribbled on the paper remained etched into her memory.

"Dad is sick. He might not have long according to the doctors. It'll be nice to have some family around. Sincerely, Susie."

Laura had spent the two days after receiving the note contemplating on whether to go see Uncle Max. She wondered who else was notified and who might show up. The decision was easy to make. Her plan was spurred on by the same blind courage she used to make all her bold and somewhat dumb decisions.

Getting into the thick of things, was the one way she could validate her life as having meaning. But this objective felt different. This time around, Laura had a positive motive driving her actions. For the first time in years, she was about to come face to face with her abuser, her demon, the devil himself, the bastard Uncle Max. Thoughts of the name suddenly left her crippled on the inside, and her movement slowed as she came to a halt.

Pam heard Laura pause, and she turned to look at her. "He isn't dead yet. You don't need to be scared."

Laura wished the lady could see through her, so she could understand just what had made her stop. Her lungs suddenly felt flattened and her knees stiff as sticks. Her nerves felt atrophied around her joints, and she could feel her pulse racing. It felt as if she had sucked in deadly air, and everything on her inside was going to shut down. Laura was about to come face to face with her past and find out just what seeing the bastard would do to her.

"This is his room," Pam said, inviting Susie and Laura in, but Laura remained outside.

"Laura," Susie called out to her cousin, who stood by the door and still refused to go in.

Her nerves, previously filled with strength and courage, had suddenly failed her. She could hear the words dancing in her mind and urging her to simply take the leap of faith into the room and confront her worst nightmare. Confronting him seemed far easier in her mind than in real life. Standing there, Laura perceived as though the air still reeked of his essence and overpowered her emotions once again.

Susie went in and barely stayed past half an hour while Laura remained seated on a bench by the wall outside. Upon hearing her cousin's footsteps, Laura raced away, searching for a restroom to try and calm her nerves. Her eyes were already tearing up badly, and her skin felt patchy with memories of his touch slowly crawling back to the surface of her mind. The air around her stung hard like the treacherous warm breath of hell breathing through his nose and down her neck as it pinned her down.

Shoving the restroom door open, Laura was consumed with an overwhelming sense of dread. Her stomach ached and her windpipe felt like it was being choked. She rushed over to the sink and splashed some water on her face.

You can do this, Laura! Take charge and bring this to an end! The voice in her head riled on.

Laura shook her head gently as she stared right back at the broken image of herself in the mirror. *I can't... God, why does this have to happen to me? I can't!*

Minutes passed as she cried aloud. She didn't care who in the world might step into the ladies' room to find her. Earlier when she had barely poked her head into his room to see the bastard's face, her stomach couldn't handle being in the same space with him again. *What was I thinking, coming here?* Allowing her emotions to get the best of her, she had lost her courage.

Digging deeper into her soul, she found a sense of confidence. *How about we do it for Tom?* The voice in her head said driving her to find another source of motivation. *The man has done everything humanly possible to love you regardless of your faults and baggage.*

The words wounded her, but she managed to somewhat dry the tears rolling down her cheeks as she slowly got up to check herself in the bathroom mirror.

Tom deserves a happy home and a happy wife. She heard the words ring aloud in her head as she splashed water onto her face one more time.

He deserves a happy home and a happy wife, she repeated the words in her head again.

"Tom deserves the best, and I can't be the best me if the devil continues to have control over my life. And, quite frankly I deserve happiness too," she said out loud as she looked at herself directly in the mirror. Then, she made her move.

Laura stormed out of the bathroom and headed back to the bastard's room. She felt strengthened and ready to face him. She was enlightened and knew exactly what she needed to do. Laura felt empowered to say the least.

Standing tall with her head held high she motioned for Susie who was standing outside in the hall.

"I have a few words I'd like to say to your father alone if you don't mind," Laura said.

Susie simply nodded. Laura took the nod as Susie's acceptance and approval. *Susie knew*, Laura thought. *She had always known.*

***

The bastard was wrinkled all over and barely able to breathe without the help of the oxygen mask placed over his face. He turned his head slowly to see Laura standing by his bedside. His stare indicated that he recognized her.

Of course, he recognized her. He made her. He hand-carved the damaged person standing before him.

"Laura," he whispered.

Laura felt something swelling in between her eyes, but she took a deep breath and held her tears back firmly. She shed every last tear she had in front of the bastard years ago, and she wasn't going to let him have the upper hand over her now. She was much stronger than that.

Laura cleared her throat and opened her mouth, "You…"

She felt her vocal cord rigidify as she struggled to accuse him of everything he had done to her. She wanted to yell out every stigma she had gone through because of him. Her emotions shut off her airways, and she struggled to breathe as the sentiments continued to swell wildly inside her. The bastard stared blankly at Laura, not one ounce of remorse showed on his face.

Laura felt her right leg move independently of her thoughts, and her body followed accordingly. Finally, she stopped just within touching distance of the monster as he continued to stare blankly at her. Her face mysteriously widened with a smile from the depths of her heart as she thought of Tom and how deserving he was of the sweet, perfect, and caring woman Samantha and Paul had raised her to be.

She wanted nothing from his tainted soul, and she certainly wanted the remainder of her life to bear the freedom her heart deserved.

Doing something she had never thought possible, Laura reached her hands out to Uncle Max. She grabbed hold of his hand and leaned closer to look directly into his eyes. He stared powerlessly at her and almost as if he was about to defecate on himself. For once, the bastard was a victim in her world, and she could see the fear in his eyes as he struggled to breathe. She made certain to savor every moment as he squinted and tried to look away. This time she was winning the psychological warfare game. She pulled his head back into position and held it into place so that he could look nowhere else but at her.

"I remember everything you did to me," she whispered into his flinching ear. "For years, I have suffered from the memories of your touch, of how you defiled me and took advantage of a child you should have protected. You are a disgusting and despicable human being."

His heart rate monitor began beeping faster and changing pitch. Laura refused to let off as she continued holding him with the same satisfying and stomach-churning smile on her face, "You sexually abused me and stole my childhood. You victimized my life for years. You chose to satisfy your dirty, sleazy addictions, and your retched actions are why I came here today."

His face grew red in fright. She stood there, holding his arm to the bed and watching him squirm in discomfort. Laura enjoyed every bit of his misery as she stood there by his bedside. Of course, what he felt in that moment didn't come close to the misery he dealt her, but it was at least something.

Laura straightened herself back up and let go of his hand, and spoke boldly, "I forgive you." With that, she turned and walked away. She never shed a single tear; he wasn't worthy of her tears.

The words released a feeling of relief through her body, unlike anything she had felt before. Her body, mind, and soul felt lighter, and the harness that burdened her fell off as she walked out of his hospital room. Passing Susie without a word, she never looked back. His evil ways had saddled her with so much anger and hatred, but she was no longer going to give him the satisfaction. He didn't deserve her forgiveness, but she knew it was what her heart needed to heal completely.

Laura exited the building with her head held high, and she could hear a choir singing beautifully in her head *this little light of mine, I'm gonna let it shine.* She started to hum the tune quietly to herself, *let it shine, let it shine, let it shine.* She envisioned her mom and dad, siblings, friends, and Tom standing together singing along with her, their strength and love had guided her the entire time.

She loved Tom as much as she knew how, but it wasn't fair that she didn't give him her entire heart. Forgiveness and letting go was the first step to being able to love Tom completely and move forward with her life. He deserved all of her, and she wanted to give it to him. The bastard would no longer have power over her, she was in control now. Finally, Laura Shirk would not be a victim anymore. She was a survivor. She would let her light shine brighter than ever.

***

Flipping through the TV stations mindlessly, Tom sipped from his glass and downed the last of his wine before hearing a noise at the front door lock. Baffled by the sound, he got to his feet cautiously, ready to act if he needed to defend himself. He steadied his breath and watched the door open slowly.

"Laura?" he sounded surprised before looking at the time. "But you…"

Laura let go of her bag and ran over to her husband and jumped on him. She trusted he would catch her as he carried her to the couch.

"I did it," she said with joy. "I confronted the bastard, I confronted Uncle Max, and I'm finally free."

Tom had known for many years of Laura's demon. Her nightmare-filled screams about the bastard had uncovered the truth despite how few details Laura shared. His heart was overjoyed that she was back home and in his arms. He sat patiently and listened for the next hour as Laura told him everything.

Getting up from the couch, Laura smiled and said to Tom, "Don't move a muscle. I have something special I've been saving for a moment like this."

Tom relaxed on the couch and watched his wife head off to change into something more comfortable. Free from her shackles, feeling strong, confident, and excited about the future, Laura couldn't wait to be with the man she loved.

THIRTY

Fall 2005

Worn out from a week working on the road, Tom pulled his car to a halt in the driveway and fumbled in his pocket for his keys. When he unlocked the front door and walked into the house, the space seemed rather silent and empty. There was not a single light on inside.

"Laura!" he called out. He hoped Laura was in the bedroom and had not heard him pull in, even though he had phoned her several hours ago.

"Laura!?" he called out again as he stood in the foyer.

The silence felt strange, and the oddity of not having his wife home where he thought she would be made him reach into his pocket for his cellphone while searching the wall to his left for the light switch. The lights came on with a single flick, and still no sign of his beloved Laura anywhere in sight.

Perplexed and worried, Tom dialed her cell and waited for it to ring with his ears pinned towards the silence in hopes of hearing something within the house. He hurried ahead, checking the kitchen quickly before hearing the ringtone from her cellphone emanate from upstairs.

"What on earth is going on?" he asked himself.

The upstairs of the house was empty as well, and he raced towards the master bedroom, wondering where she could be on the night he had assured her he was returning home. Usually, Laura would be waiting happily in the living room to greet him when he returned from a work trip, and it was even odder that she wasn't picking up his calls.

His hand still pinned against his ear as he traced the ringing cellphone, Tom whispered with the door inches from his hand, "Laura! Are you in there?"

He nudged the door open gently and heard it creak as it took forever to reveal the inside of the room. Frustrated by the darkness and pretty much eager to see if his wife was simply asleep before he called the cops, he flicked on the lights and saw Laura lying half-naked in a sea of rose petals on their bed.

For Laura, it was truly a blessed thing to share her love fully with her husband. No longer a victim but a survivor, she yearned for him while he was gone. Laura never thought she would emotionally get to a place where she could feel true love and comfort being intimate with a man. Oh, but she did indeed. Fully exposed with her heart wide open, she trusted and loved Tom. He was her soulmate, her partner for life.

Purring as he kicked off his shoes, "You sneaky girl," he whispered.

The sweet and alluring scent of lavender filled the air, and he could smell the freshly washed Egyptian cotton sheets under the fragrant red roses. She was as sly as ever, and he had somehow forgotten what she was capable of. The love of his life, ever so filled with surprises and knowing just too well how to get his motor running, lay on the bed with just a thong around her waist and Victoria's Secret bra he had given her for Valentine's Day.

Smiling brightly, with her glossed lips beckoning for him to come closer, while she motioned to him with her finger.

"Hello, honey," she whispered in sonorous words cascading beautifully into his ears and setting his mind ablaze.

She was perfectly tanned and looking like a goddess sent to get him. Tom chuckled excitedly and leaped onto his side of the bed as they both stared at each other.

Setting on the nightstand just by the bedside were a bottle of champagne and some strawberries.

"Babe," he whispered. "Did you miss me?"

Laura purred, placed a finger to his lips, and silenced her handsome husband from speaking. Tom watched his seductive wife, whose olive skin, scented wonderfully, reached over his shoulder and handpick a single strawberry. She slid it in between his lips and slowly leaned closer to lock hers with his and share a slow but perfect bite from the fruit together.

The soft brush from her lips sent his entire soul tingling, while he could feel himself begin to respond from within. Reaching for her shoulder and running his fingers slowly down her body until he found her curvy buttocks, he smiled, grabbed hold of her, and pulled her closer.

Laura smiled and whispered, "Did you miss me?"

Nodding his head gently and smiling, he replied, "Badly babe. Badly."

She believed him, for his words never bore lies, and his eyes sparkled of the truth. She locked her gaze on his lips and found herself coveting them. Like two minds functioning as one, Tom leaned closer, meeting his wife halfway. They teased each other softly with their warm breaths merging before the fleshy pair of lips fused as one and savored the wonderful taste.

Laura moaned softly while Tom reached for the back of her head to pull her close. He had not realized just how much he missed his wife's lips and having them trapped between his, he couldn't help but want never to let go. He drew his breath in to savor the moment.

Digging her fingers into the sheets and yanking at them as his tongue continued to set her body on fire, Laura moaned, "I missed you." Every fiber in her body cried for his touch, and every inch of her begged to feel him. Laura's soul yearned for one man and one alone. Tom. Laura looked up and into her husband's eyes with a raised brow, grinning to alert him of what would come next.

The full blue moon still watched, a silent witness to their lovemaking.

EPILOGUE

G leaming beautifully into the room, the sun settled its golden rays atop her face as she slowly dragged herself into consciousness. She was still with her back to the bed and her eyes staring at the ceiling as they had done some hours ago, in the middle of the night. Laura smiled and sighed softly. She was truly happy.

Thankfully, the air smelled better and fresher in spring, just as she liked it. The brightly colored walls warmed her heart as did the two smiling faces captured in beautiful moments of joy. Picture frames filled with images of her two children hung all over the room. The images bore a striking resemblance to her husband laying on the other side of the bed. Everything was as it should be. Laura couldn't ask for anything more.

Her eyes fell upon the brown rimmed frame hanging on the wall, as she tossed around in the king-sized bed she shared with the man who mattered most in her life. The frame was hanging just inches from a large portrait of their entire family. The contents were a poem she knew by heart and would recite with delight whenever she remembered the story behind it.

Tom had given it to her when they were young. The words had sentimental value and stood as a testament to his love for her. The poem assured her that he would always seek ways to express his love, be it through words or actions. Laura stared at the framed reminder for a while and sighed happily. Reminiscing of the memories it had brought back from when he recited the words the night he asked her to marry him.

The morning felt perfect until she reached her hand a little farther from her body, she hoped to pat Tom's lovely buttocks, but she couldn't find it. Laura turned away from the pictures on the wall with widened eyes, she wondered if this moment was another dream.

Indeed, she looked to her other side where he was sound asleep, purring gently. He remained the best thing that had ever happened to Laura but not the only thing. The children soon came barging into the room with their arms parted widely and their faces beaming with joy as they screamed out for their parents'.

"Mommy!" Emma cried aloud before climbing on the bed and wrapping her arms around Laura's neck.

She welcomed the gorgeous girl with beautifully flowing brunette hair into her bed before planting a kiss on her cheek. Her heart was full of grace and thanks as she took a moment to admire the young girl staring intensely into her green eyes that reminded her so much of Samantha. She remembered the brilliance Samantha exuded, which, without a doubt, was now in her daughter. Emma giggled and tucked her arms around her mother some more while Ethan poked at Tom a bit.

Ethan, impatient that his dad still hadn't woken up, leaped towards his sleeping father, and yanked his feet until Tom mumbled incoherently, "Oh! Good morning, I guess it's time to get up!"

Laura laughed, as did Emma and Ethan, who tickled their daddy and had him sitting up within seconds. Tom rubbed his eyes clean of sleep and yawned aloud while Ethan found himself space to sit between his parents as he played with his father's chin. Laura stared at the reddish blonde-haired boy who bore striking resemblance to Tom in almost every way. Running his fingers through Ethan's hair, Tom held his breath and sighed aloud as he turned to look at his ladies.

Looking at his son with sleepy eyes, Tom yawned and asked Laura, "Babe, is it morning already?"

"It's, morning honey."

"Good morning, babe."

She replied immediately, "Good morning, honey."

Seeking attention, Ethan greeted his father, "Good morning, daddio," while Laura braided Emma's hair.

Emma enjoyed such moments with Laura, for now, at least. Eventually, she would be too old for her mother to do her hair, Laura would savor the moments while they lasted. Ethan looked over at her, bearing a somewhat envious look, he was a Momma's boy.

"Oh, I see someone is getting jealous!" Tom chuckled before sneaking his arms around his son and pulling him closer.

Ethan forced a smile and shrugged, but he was no match for Tom, who scooped the little fella off from the bed and set him atop his thighs before raking his fingers through his hair and responding, "A good morning to you too, buddy. Thanks for waking me up this early by the way".

Ethan laughed, smiled, and stared at Emma, who seemed to have been in on the idea of getting their parents up early in the morning. Tom and Laura shot each other a brief stare before leaning closer and sharing a quick kiss.

"So, what do you little nuggets want this morning?" Tom asked the kids with a raised brow.

Emma shrugged gently while her brother did the same.

"Mom promised us cakes," Emma noted. Cakes were short for pancakes in their house.

It was typical Emma, food first before anything else. She would have her pick of everything and clean up without leaving anything to waste. Laura often wondered if she was blessed with the trait from her or Tom, but regardless, she was healthy and fit as a fiddle which meant they were more than happy to oblige her.

Emma continued, "But I want dad to make us big breakfast like he always does. Yummy big breakfast!"

Ethan laughed but supported the idea. Weekends were Emma's favorite, and food played a big part in it since her father made them breakfast, and they hung out together in the morning. Tom looked at Laura with a smile. Cooking was his thing and he loved to make "big breakfast," as their daughter always called it.

Laura shook her head and laughed. It was those mornings, when they were all together, that she loved him the most. As she looked at Emma and Ethan, she turned and spoke to Tom.

"Thank you for everything. Thanks for being the best husband ever."

Tom smiled, his blood rushed to his cheeks and his eyes held a drop of tear in the corners. He leaned closer to Laura and placed his lips onto hers, he held her tighter savoring her lips as they threatened to melt away between his. They soon broke apart upon as they noticed Emma staring at them momentarily before averting her gaze as she stewed.

Emma rolled her eyes and mumbled underneath her breath, "That is just gross. You two flirting weirds me out."

"Sorry, baby," Laura reached for her little girl and palmed her hair gently with her hand. "Mommy needs some Daddy loving too."

Laura smiled and kissed Tom briefly before he hopped away joyously doing his odd but hilarious dance. She stared out the window momentarily at the sunrise, barely peeking through the darkness. As night had changed into day, so did a light shine on how times had changed, how far she had come, and how much she had overcome.

She had managed to speak her truth, she had learned to love herself, and she had learned to allow herself to be truly vulnerable with the man she loved. She loved him with her whole heart and the feeling was truly amazing. The past certainly impacted the person she had become, and she remained grateful for every new day.

Laura felt like the happiest woman in the world. She closed her eyes and felt tears roll down her cheeks as she soaked in the picture she had painted so beautifully.

Letting go of the secrets she concealed, created beauty from ashes.

A Note From The Author

Thank you for reading The Secrets We Conceal. This was my debut novel, but my second novel is already in the works and I am looking forward to writing several more. If you enjoyed this book, please consider leaving an honest review on your favorite store.

Writing hasn't been my career, my degree is in mathematics, and I have spent the last 20+ years in business. I had a story to tell, so I decided to tell it. The journey was challenging, emotional, and downright scary at times, but in the end, it was incredibly rewarding.

It was important to me to write this book to spread awareness about child sexual abuse. For so long this topic has been uncomfortable, something you just don't talk about. You don't sit down for coffee and say hey I'm a survivor of child sex abuse. Typically, when you do mention it, you can feel the listener squirming with discomfort. It isn't easy to discuss. If my book helps one person along their personal survival journey, the hard work and effort put into writing the book will be worth it.

For mothers and fathers reading the book, know that it is okay to talk about this topic with your children. Open lines of communication can go a long way in giving your child a safe space if they need it. Sometimes they need a little nudge to open up about their abuse, it is difficult for a child to put into words.

To the victims out there – you are a survivor! IT IS NOT YOUR FAULT! You didn't do anything wrong. Don't be afraid to talk to someone, there are a lot of resources out there now. SPEAK! FORGIVE! HEAL! Know that you deserve the best life has to offer, be willing and able to allow yourself to receive it. It is okay to not be okay. It is okay to ask for help!

www.rainn.org is an amazing resource. I encourage you to check it out. If you need help or know someone who needs help you can also contact 800-656-HOPE

Out of 1000 sexual assaults, approximately only 310 are reported to the police. Many children wait to report or never report child sexual abuse.

Important statistics on child sexual abuse.

- 1 in 4 girls and 1 and 13 boys experience child sexual abuse in some way during their childhood.
- 82% of all victims under 18 are female.
- Females 16-19 are 4 times more likely than the general population to be victims of rape, attempted rape, or sexual assault.

- 90% of cases go unreported

The effects of child sexual abuse can be long-lasting and affect the victim's thought, acts, and feelings over a lifetime. Resulting in short-term and long-term physical and emotional health consequences. Victims are more likely than non-victims to experience the following mental health challenges.

- About 4 times more likely to develop symptoms of drug abuse
- About 4 times more like to experience PTSD as adults
- About 3 times more likely to experience a major depressive episode as adults
- Chronic conditions later in life, such as heart disease, obesity, and cancer
- Increased risk for suicide or suicide attempts
- More like to engage in risky sexual behaviors or sex with multiple partners

Perpetrators of Child Sexual Abuse are often related to the Victim

- 88% of CPS sexual abuse claims find the perpetrator is male. 9% of cases are female, and 3% are unknown.
- 91% of child sexual abuse is perpetrated by someone the child or child's family knows.

Another outcome commonly associated with child sexual abuse is an increased risk of re-victimization throughout a person's life. For example, recent studies have found:

- Females exposed to child sexual abuse are at 2-13 times increased risk of sexual victimization in adulthood.

- Individuals who experienced child sexual abuse are at twice the risk for non-sexual intimate partner violence.

Resources – www.rainn.org and www.cdc.gov

ACKNOWLEDGEMENTS

To Chris, who has always been my biggest supporter. You stand by my side through it all, you are my life partner and I appreciate you more than words can express. Our family means the world to me. Thank you for the late-night chats and book discussions. Thank you for reading several versions of the book and taking this journey with me.

To my children, I love you. Thank you for putting up with mommy's late nights and early mornings while I worked to finish the book. Everything I do is for you. You will do great things someday and I am proud of you always. Thank you for your genuine excitement and pride that mommy wrote a book.

To my dad, thank you. Thank you for teaching me to go after my dreams and never be afraid to fail. You have always been my number one fan. Barb, thanks for loving my dad and taking such good care of him.

To my mom in heaven, thank you for being an example of a strong woman. Thank you for teaching me not to accept anything less than my best. I miss you every day, but I know you are smiling down on all of us.

To my sisters and brothers, Danielle, Dave, Al, and Jen. Thank you for always looking after me, calling me out on my shit, and pushing me to be a better person. Thank you for always being there for your lil' sis. I have the best siblings in the world. I couldn't have done this without your support.

Steph "Cuddy" Della Costa, thank you for joining me on this adventure. You are a cherished lifelong friend who has always been there for me. I appreciate your guidance and discussion throughout this process and your attention to detail regarding the book. You gave me a safe place to talk through the process, I appreciate you.

To my friends and co-workers, you have been a great support system, encouraging me along the way and cheering me on, when I thought I might chicken out. You are truly amazing people, and I am grateful to have you in my life.

To my editorial team, there are several of you and you know who you are. You helped bring the story to life. Your guidance and patience were a blessing. Thank you for taking such care with my work.

Thank you to the amazing team at The Paper House who helped guide me through the publishing process. I couldn't have done it without you.

ABOUT THE AUTHOR

Born and raised a Yankee who loves NY-style pizza and Philly cheesesteaks. I was introduced to the amazing world of Southern BBQ after moving to Tennessee where I live with my husband and two children. My family is my main priority, everything I do is for them. I attended college in the '90s and received a degree in mathematics with a minor in secondary education, I went on to coach cheerleading and dance for 20 years and won a Hip Hop Dance World Championship. Anything and everything creative is my absolute favorite, so writing has always been a hobby. When I'm writing, I like to wife hard, mom hard, paint, read good books and watch good movies.

You can learn more about S.R. Fabrico by visiting her website www.srfabrico.com or following her on social media IG: @srfabrico_author and FB: @srfabricoauthor

Topics And Questions For Discussion

1. Are there any quotes or passages from the book that stood out to you and why? What did you like or not like about them? How did they impact you personally?

2. Why do you think Laura chose not to tell anyone about her abuse? Do you think she made the wrong choice? What difference would it have made, if any? How would you handle her situation?

3. What experiences did you have in middle school? Could you relate to Laura's experiences?

4. What personality traits do you think Laura acquired throughout the book because of her past?

5. How is womanhood explored throughout the novel? How does Laura navigate her years into womanhood? Do you think she could have done anything differently?

6. Discuss Laura's relationship with Tom? How does he help her heal? How does he understand Laura? Is Tom a good partner for Laura? Why or why not?

7. Discuss your feelings for Uncle Max? What kind of person was he? How did he impact not just Laura's life but Susie's and Aunt Penny's lives?

8. What do you think life was like for Susie and Aunt Penny? Did they know what was going on? Were they victims themselves?

9. Do you think Laura got her justice? She forgives Uncle Max for what he did to her,

10. How did this make you feel? Would you have done the same thing? Why or why not? How you would have addressed Uncle Max if you were in Laura's shoes?

11. Were you surprised by any parts of the book? If so which parts and why?

12. Who would you cast in the movie The Secrets We Conceal?

13. If you could talk to the author, what questions would you ask?